WILL YOU KNOW MY NAME?

Souls Adrift, volume 1

J. A. Dege

Annie
Thanks for always
being an inspiration
and a rock of Gibraltar
for all of us!
-

This is a work of fiction. Any references to historical events, real people, or real locales, though meticulously researched, are used within fictitious parameters.

ISBN-13: 978-1-7336628-1-9

Cover Photo by: Elijah Hiett
Cover design by: J.A. Dege
Library of Congress Control Number: 2018675309
Printed in the United States of America

To those who believe, one way or another...

This book is dedicated to my father who thought it perfectly normal for the entire family to appear at the dinner table with books in hand.

To Gene Sites - I can still smell your pipe, my friend.

A special Thank You for all the love and support of fellow authors of the Twitter Tribe. To friends and family for their support and enthusiasm. To Adam Eccles for the Tech nudges. This book would still be only a dream without all of you.

CONTENTS

IN THE BEGINNING...

Perspective is everything.

As children we learn some version of the truth, or at least the truth our ancestors believed. Some say life on Earth was the product of evolution, while others espouse the belief that a god created Earth and everything on it. Many explanations were handed down through the generations of human life, some prevailed, some conflicted, some were lost – forgotten in time or forgotten by design.

The Soul who maintained Earth's Program took up that burden when comparatively few souls had chosen to reside on the newly created planet. On Earth, his role was once labeled by many humans as God, under various Names and Guises. He liked the term as it was short and simple, easy for him, as well as the humans, to remember. He let the humans sort it out on their own. His role as he saw it, was the Caretaker.

His strength lay in the vitality of the collective of souls scattered across the universe. If one was lost, his power to manipulate the Programs diminished. The Programs were designed to protect and nurture the souls. It was his job, and that of his fellow Guardians, to see that the Programs on each planet functioned properly.

More than two thousand years ago, the human population on Earth grew quarrelsome, fractured, and unbalanced. Human nature evolved contrary to the Program. The swift brutality of the human clashes freed too many souls from their corporeal forms. Many were lost, their life force fading before retrieval by the Guardians was possible.

The Caretaker came to Earth to investigate the cause of the strife, but what he found was almost more than he could manage, taxing his strength to the very edge of his own existence. He created a new soul, an heir, before he diminished beyond the strength required for such an act. And yet he still needed time for that soul to mature, to be trained for its inheritance. The Caretaker opted to merge with other souls, risking the incorporation of their identities and memories with his own, in order to maintain his ability to control the Program. What his heir endured during his short lifespan on Earth, shook the Caretaker's faith in human nature.

Two thousand years later, the new Caretaker, Joshua, was still trying to sort out the darkness.

ON THE FIRST DAY...

Friday July 3 – evening

Julia Altieri visited her grandmother at the Shining Hope Nursing Home faithfully every evening when her shift ended at the clinic. The elderly woman lay quiet, no longer agitated, the drugs keeping her in a trance-like state. The nurse had combed her white hair and dressed her in a lilac-print nightgown. Gran lost the ability to speak six months back, but deep-down Julia believed her grandmother could still hear her, still make sense of her words. She told Gran about her day, the patients, the traffic, her nightmares and dreams. There's no one else to listen to me, Julia thought, and Gran has no one else who comes to visit. *Would she miss me? Will I see her again? Or Mom? Dad?* Once again, Julia found herself wondering about the real nature of existence, wondering if there was in fact any kind of afterlife.

Julia held her grandmother's hand between

hers, wishing for one last moment of real contact. She laid her forehead on their joined hands and spoke so softly only her grandmother would be able to hear her. “Gran, I am so sorry. I can’t keep up, I’m so deep in debt I’m drowning in it. They’ll take care of you. In the new place. I don’t know what else to do.” She stopped, kissed the hand she held, and then choked back tears as she slipped out of the room unnoticed.

Julia walked with mechanical footsteps toward her apartment. Those fourteen blocks were the longest of her life. Wiping tears from her eyes, she looked up in the sky and directed her thoughts upward. *I’m sorry, Dad, I can’t do this anymore.* Her car repossessed, living paycheck to paycheck with little left over after rent, utilities, and Gran’s monthly fee. *I hate it here. This city, this life.* Julia made herself focus on her whereabouts, pivoted and continued in the direction of the river instead of home.

Eleven o’clock at night, no notice was taken of a slim young woman with long blond hair walking slowly along Cedar Avenue out onto the center of the bridge. No one cared. It wasn’t only that people were indifferent, there just was no one *to* care. Julia stood a long time staring at the night sky, and the river below, but mostly she was seeing images flash through her mind and feeling the crushing weight of her fucked up life dragging her into a suffocating abyss. *Damned if I do, damned if I don’t,* she thought, and meant it. She climbed over the bridge railing and sat down on the narrow lip overhanging the river. Her feet dangled over the edge. Her scuffed Rockport boots were outlined by the rolling black water. The stars shone bright, the moon was a mere crescent, just enough light to cast glints off her blond hair. Hidden by the guardrail, she remained poised on the edge while cars slipped by behind her, ignorant of her presence. Ignorant of her state of mind.

"Twenty-seven years old and I can't do this anymore. I'm sorry, Gran," she said to the night sky. She exhaled sharply and cast her line into the wind before her. "This is the end of my rope." She pushed off and fell into the river below. A muffled splash, and her body was swept into the current, her last tears mingling with the murky waters.

Friday July 3 – late night

City of Eagan, MN – Medical Examiner Log:

7:28 AM - Male, Caucasian, approximately 42 years of age, DOA. Cause of death - exsanguination; both wrists severed vertically. Notifying next of kin. Toxicology ordered.

8:43 AM – Female, Hispanic, DOB 7/2/1978, DOA. Cause of death - unknown, toxicology ordered. Next of kin being investigated.

9:18 AM – Male, African American, 37 years of age, DOA. Cause of death – gunshot wound to head, self-inflicted. Next of kin reported body.

9:46 AM – Female, Caucasian, 41 years of age, DOA. No visible cause of death, suspected poisoning, possible drug over-dose. Toxicology pending.

10:01 AM – Male, Caucasian, approximately 45-50 years of age, no ID. Cause of death - drowning.

10:22 AM – Male, African American, approx. 40 years of age,

no ID. Cause of death - impact, fell from...

The rescue squad volunteer, John Stapleton, took his coffee to the office of his friend, Dr. Sam Watson, the Dakota County Medical Examiner.

"Sam?" he called out as he entered. Sam waved him in as he finished signing yet another death certificate. John had the log book in his hand. He'd been reading it while he filled his go-cup with fresh brew. "Don't you think all these suicides a little odd? Not the usual suspects, so to speak."

Sam looked up over the rim of his glasses and nodded. "It's been going on for weeks, months even."

"What the hell?" John looked back through the log, shaking his head. Entries dated back to the beginning of the year and only a few were elderly dying in nursing homes, a few auto crash victims and the like. Most of the entries ruled suicides committed by men and women between the ages of thirty and fifty. Not the usual age group at all.

John's radio squawked. He forgot his coffee on Sam's desk.

THE SECOND DAY…

Saturday July 4 – morning

Michael and Gabriel waited outside The Office. They were supposed to be in the middle of the morning briefing. Gabriel leaned against the wall, trying to hide his impatience.

Michael paced.

Azrael joined them, yawning. "This week's been a blur. So many suicides I can hardly reach them all before it's too late to pull them out. Lost a few souls, irretrievably. Damn it all."

"Hell of a week," Michael agreed.

"Devil's agents win this round," Azrael said, scrubbing his face with his hands, trying in vain to rouse himself.

"Will you two quit with the jokes? It's not funny. I think you're both spending a little too much time among the humans." Gabriel tried to look annoyed, but he was too worried. "Joshua have a plan?" He met the eyes of the other two, apprehension filling his own. His worry increased when neither answered. "If anyone can get the measure of this mess, it's Joshua."

Michael nodded. "I don't know though. He was pretty messed up last night when the numbers started coming in. He mentioned pulling out and starting over on a new planet. Just letting this generation continue to their inevitable end. Retrieve them as they go."

"This has to be hard on him," Gabriel said.

Michael had been spending much of his time consulting with Joshua about the current situation on Earth and knew the toll it was taking on him. They needed to find a solution. And hope the situation didn't deteriorate any further before they found it.

It was odd to be left waiting outside The Office. Joshua usually had an open-door policy. Michael finally knocked on the door and was surprised when Uriel opened it to them and beckoned them in.

"We've got a problem," Uriel said.

"Where's Joshua?" Michael asked. A slight frown creased his brow.

Uriel simply pointed to a note on the desk. They all approached to read it.

"I don't know if I can fix this, but I must try. I'm going down to Earth. Back soon. -J"

Michael was the first to finish reading.

Michael was shaken. And furious. "Uriel, you let him leave without consulting the rest of us?"

"He was gone when I got here, Michael," Uriel said.

"Do we know which form he took? Did he take a tracking unit?" Gabriel asked.

Uriel shrugged and shook his head. "I don't know any more than you."

Michael's hand holding the note began to shake. His face lost all color. He closed his eyes, drew in a deep, calming breath, and slowly let it out. It did nothing to calm him. "Oh, holy hell! This note is all the planning he put into this idea. What are we going to do?"

Uriel shook his grizzled head, and turned bleak yet hopeful eyes to Azrael.

Azrael ran a hand over his shaved black hair and shook his head. "Don't look at me. It was a wonder we found him last time he went AWOL."

*****

Joshua's feet touched Earth as he materialized. His body shuddered as full feeling returned. Anticipation, excitement, and yes, he'd admit it, a twinge of fear swept through his corporeal form. He looked down at his physical body, flexed his arms and fingers. *Haven't lost anything, everything seems in working order*. He tried to remember the last time he dematerialized to travel. It had been a while, a long while. He remembered to control his radiance and reel in the energy emanating from him.

Just had to pretend he was human. Done it before. Not that hard.

I can do this.

He walked along the shore of the river and thought, *I'll figure it out as I go. Wing it! Improvise.*

Oh hell, I don't know what to do.

That's why it's called improvising, you idiot.

He continued walking, following the electronic beeps on his wrist unit.

He found the girl's body beside the river, washed up between some rocks. He swept his eyes around the area, making sure no other humans were about. His eyes continued searching. *I hope I got here soon enough*. Souls usually remained near the body for a little while, unless one of Azrael's assistants came to escort it. He closed his eyes and just listened. He didn't need to track it. He sensed an errant soul, picked up the unique vibration and harmonic melody. *Yes, it's still here*. Opening his eyes, he finally spied it hovering behind some shrubbery overhanging the river bank.

An intense shapeshifting glow, pulsing with energy, was softly humming, ebbing and flowing. He sensed its hesitation. It was inquisitive and studying him. Quivering with indecision, its harmonics went up the scale a chord or two. Joshua crouched down on bent knees, laid one hand on the girl's body and gestured with the other to the soul, beckoning, encouraging it to approach. He remained as still as possible while the soul cautiously drifted in closer.

Careful, do not want to spook it.

He held his breath as the soul drew nearer. When it eased over him, enveloping him, he felt a soft electrical charge while it examined him. Curiosity, confusion, recognition, and a soft gentleness registered in Joshua's mind. He smiled at the surge of positivity coursing through him, giving him a much-needed jolt of energy.

I think it likes me.

Slowly the soul slid down his arm, slipped through his open fingertips and re-entered the girl's body. Thus, without really thinking too much about it, he brought the girl back to life. He questioned what he'd done. Should he have interfered? Didn't know. *The truth is, I'm tired of careful plans and structuring lives.* None of it was working.

Earth's a fucking mess.

Joshua watched a look of dread come over the girl's face when she opened her eyes and recognized her surroundings.

"What did you do?" she whispered as she sat up.

"I brought you back." Joshua leaned closer to her to observe. *Wow.* He was actually speaking with a human. He tried to recall the last time, settled on 1917, no 1918. The end of the Great War, they called it. France. The nurse. A wave of sadness unsettled him.

The girl slammed both of her hands against his chest and knocked him over. "Why?! Why would you do that?" she screamed at him and rose to her feet.

Joshua uprighted himself onto his knees. *Ow. That actually hurt.* He stood up, dusting dirt and grass off his backside and knees. "I need answers."

"You what?!" Her expression was incredulous. And outraged. Her face was flushed, eyes flashing.

Oblivious, still swiping off debris, Joshua asked, "Why did you end your life?"

"Unbelievable. Un-fucking believable." She began walking back to the bridge. "What do you care?" she threw over her shoulder and kept climbing.

Joshua remained frozen in place, his mouth hanging open. What the hell? What just happened here? "Wait! Where are you going?" He scrambled to follow her.

"To try again."

Joshua chased her. Reaching the bridge, he saw her begin to climb over the guardrail. Again. He skidded to a stop only a few feet away, afraid to get too close. "No, don't. Please." Disbelief was written on his face and bled into his voice. Such a sweet, playful soul. Why is she throwing this life away? "You don't want to do this."

"Why not?" Their eyes met. "Look around you. This world sucks. Sucks the life right out of you. Are you frickin' blind?" Her voice was accusatory, but it shook. From anger at her lot in life, anger at this stupid guy who resuscitated her back into it, and from sheer weariness. She'd given up. And he just fucked up her suicide. Asshole.

"Please, come back over here." He said it softly, not yet understanding why he needed her to remain, to stay alive. He looked at the sprawling city around them, the immense infrastructure which had evolved out of a far simpler plan. Definitely not the result he had expected. He really had let his attention wander away from this planet. "Please, just give me another chance," he whispered barely loud enough for her to hear.

She frowned at his words, not understanding his meaning. "Who the hell are you?"

He hesitated, uncertain how to answer her. *What should I tell her? The truth? Or what she can understand?* Resolving not to blow her mind, nor get involved in a lengthy explanation, he chose a construct of her world. One of the titles Earth's people had created to explain his role on their planet. The short one. "I am God." He met her eyes and held his breath. The first reaction was always the most important.

She looked at him, saw only an ordinary man. Longish brown hair, green eyes, average sort of guy in jeans and tennis shoes. Her eyes returned to his. "I always imagined God with brown eyes." She watched as his green eyes suddenly appeared brown.

Joshua held her eyes while he listened to her mind processing. Honesty was always the best policy, right? As she began to sway a little, he changed his mind. Perhaps not. "Please. I want to understand why Earth has gone to hell. I want to fix it."

"If you *are* God, you should already know. All this injustice, suffering, discrimination? Who needs a God that allows this? You? You can't fix this."

*****

Gabriel rushed into The Office where he found Michael reading reports on multiple screens. "Azrael thinks he's located him."

Michael could not keep the skepticism from his face. It had taken them months to find Joshua the last time he took off on them. To find him on the same day... Not bloody likely.

"There's a reported suicide/resurrection in London. It has to be him!" Gabriel said.

"I don't know –" Michael began.

Gabriel waved away Michael's objections. "Never underestimate the power of Azrael."

"Isn't that supposed to be 'the Power of God'?" Michael asked, shaking his head. He sighed in utter frustration. "We master the teeming chaos and shape the infrastructures of worlds. And created the humans. And now Joshua's down there among them. Alone."

"Are you with me, or not?" Gabriel asked. "We've got to go. Now. You know what he's capable of on his own."

Azrael ran into the office carrying a portable tablet. "Got another possible in Minneapolis. Central North America."

"Fine," Michael said, throwing his hands up. "Fine!" Wild goose chasing, here we go. Again. He took the coordinates from Azrael. "I've got the one in Minneapolis. You two, go to London."

*****

Michael arrived on the Cedar Avenue bridge and looked around him. The Minnesota River flowed beneath his feet. He heard a splash and turned in that direction in time to see Joshua in his usual physical form plunge off the bridge.

"No!" Michael dodged cars on his way to the other side of the bridge. Leaning over the guardrail, he saw two people in the water. One floating. The other was flailing and bobbing and sputtering. "He can't swim!" Michael yelled down to the other person in the water.

The girl floated on her back, waiting for the rapids to take her to oblivion. Again. When she heard shouting, she pulled her head up out of the water. Looking up, she saw a man waving his arms frantically and pointing down at her. No, not *at* her. Near her. Oh, hell. The crazy guy jumped, too. Then she made sense of the words the guy was shouting at her.

"Why'd he follow me in then?" she yelled back. She had uprighted herself and automatically started treading water.

"No idea!" Michael yelled down. "Quick! He's slipping under again."

"Oh, for the love of God. Are you fucking kidding me?" She swam over to the guy who was still flailing and now, drifting downriver. "For Christ's sake, calm down, you idiot. I'll save you. Stop fighting me!" she said as she began towing him toward the shore. "Jeez, it's hard enough fighting the current. Relax, for the love of God! I'm not going to let you drown."

A few minutes later, Joshua lay on the river bank coughing up water and trying to catch his breath at the same time. Not an easy task, he was finding out the hard way. *I have to learn how to swim.* And he needed to remember the rules were a little different down here.

"So much for walking on water," the girl muttered. She was sitting beside him, swiping her long, wet hair from her eyes and face. She turned on him. "What the hell were you thinking?"

"I was trying to –" He stopped, coughed, and hacked more water up. "I was trying to save you. Again, I might add."

"That guy up there said you can't swim." She pointed to the man now scrambling down from the bridge.

Joshua looked up to see Michael working his way down the bank. "Aw, hell. He found me. That was fast." He lay back down, spent. This day is going well, he thought. So much for fixing this by himself. *Improvise, my ass*. Another fit of coughing shook him. *I am such an idiot.*

Michael slid to a stop in front of the two sopping wet people. He looked down at Joshua, and offered him a hand up. "You know you freak everyone out when you take off like this!"

"Is he your keeper? 'Cause you sure need one," the girl said, getting to her feet.

"No," Michael said abruptly, hardly noticing her.

"He thinks he is," Joshua replied. He turned to Michael. "I left a note."

Michael let an exasperated sigh leave him. "Minus a hell of a lot of detail!"

"Pfft, details. Lot of good they've been doing us. Wait. Where'd the girl go?" Joshua suddenly noticed she was no longer standing with them. "We have to follow her. She might try it again." He caught sight of her climbing the grassy slope near the top of the bank, almost to the road. He scrambled after her once again.

Michael hesitated a moment on the river bank, gripping his windblown black hair, trying to make sense of Joshua's actions. *Oh, holy hell. The guys would kill me if I lost him now.*

"You can't stay here. You need to go back... up," Michael said when he caught up to Joshua. "I've got Uriel working with Christian on the numbers and the projected outcomes. We'll figure something out."

"Uriel's not good with numbers. And we've been working the numbers. The numbers aren't good, Michael, and you know it!" Joshua was walking as fast as he could, trying not to lose sight of the girl. He was relieved when she turned away from the bridge. They were walking through some sort of shopping district. He pulled up short. He'd always wanted to go shopping. He looked longingly at the shops, then collected himself. *Don't get distracted. Follow the girl.* "Michael, hurry! She's getting away." He ran to catch her.

Michael growled in exasperation. "Fine. Fine!" He ran after Joshua.

Joshua called out to the girl. "Wait, please."

She stopped. *Crap, he said 'please'.* Her parents raised her to be polite. She raised her eyes to the sky, seeking strength. And patience. To deal with a couple of crazies. She whirled around. "Why are you following me? You found your friend. Or he found you. Whatever. Just go... play... somewhere."

"You're angry with me." Joshua tilted his head. "Why are you angry with me? I don't understand."

"Your eyes are green again." Wow, that was kind of freaky, she thought. She hadn't seen him switch out contacts either time. What the hell?

"Sorry. You preferred brown, right?" Joshua shifted his eyes to brown a second time. "Better?"

She stared with her mouth open, a wave of dizziness hit her. "I think I better eat something. Soon." She turned from the two men and began walking toward the entry of her apartment building. It was an older unit, not entirely crappy but showing signs of sliding off the scale. Of melting into the pavement and being scraped away by bulldozers. She keyed in her entry code and thought she'd made her escape. Turning back, she saw the two men right on her heels, the original crazy guy's hand on the door. “Seriously? You think I’m going to just let you waltz into my apartment?”

Joshua stopped in his tracks. “I think the polite thing to do is ask, right?” He looked at her with sincerity and a sort of lost puppy look. A puppy with warm brown eyes. “May we come in?”

She shook her head at herself. “Fine. Come in. I gotta be as crazy as you two.” Dry clothes, eat something, and then she needed some serious-ass sleep. She led them up to the third floor and opened her door with the key she kept on a lanyard. And somehow managed not to lose after jumping in the river. Twice, for fuck’s sake. “Please, do come in,” she said. “I wasn’t expecting company, forgive the mess.” She didn’t mean it. She could care less what they thought of her home. It was a small apartment with kitchen, dining, and living rooms combined, one bedroom, and a closet of a bathroom. Two total windows overlooked the alley and the grocery store. “Make yourselves comfortable. I’m getting dry clothes.”

She stepped into the bedroom and leaned against the closed door. Reaching behind, she locked it. *I can’t believe I just let two nut-cases into my apartment. Maybe if I feed them, they’ll go away?* No, you don’t feed strays. They never leave. She shook her head at herself again.

She dropped her wet clothes in a basket and stepped into dry jeans and an old Prince t-shirt, a trophy from her mother’s closet years ago. Returning to the main room, she found them arguing in quiet tones. They stopped when they noticed her. "Oh, hey, don't mind me. You two figure out where you're going next?" She continued to the kitchen, from the cupboard she drew out a loaf of white bread and a jar of creamy peanut butter. She was busy making herself a sandwich when she noticed they were just watching her. Silent. She looked at both of their mesmerized faces. "Hungry?"

"No," Michael said.

"Yes," Joshua said, more out of politeness than remembering what the word meant.

"Do you two ever agree on anything?" she asked.

"No," Michael said.

"He's right on that one." Joshua grinned at Michael's frown. His stomach growled, loudly. "What was that?" he asked, bewilderment scribbled all over his face.

She looked at him, then Michael, whose face was just as bewildered. Her mind was grinding words out slowly. *These. Two. Are. Starting. To. Creep. Me. Out.* "That was your stomach."

"Which means?" A look of panic crossed Joshua's face. You forget some of the details when it's been a hundred years or so away from a planet.

She stared at him. "Are you for real?" She watched as he began patting himself all over, and then nodded back to her. *Wow. I wonder if I can even explain this if I dial 911.* "It means, yes, you are hungry. Would you like a peanut butter sandwich?"

"Is that what you are having?" Joshua came

closer to observe. He sniffed the air above the slice of bread covered in peanut butter. "That smells... good." He took it from her after she placed another slice of bread on top and handed it to him. He held it while watching her assemble another.

"Are you sure you don't want one?" she asked Michael.

"I didn't think we would be intruding this long." He gave Joshua his best *What the Hell Are We Doing Here?* look. "But it does smell good. Thank you."

Michael took the second sandwich from her. He also held onto it, watching her make another for herself. When she finished and took a large bite out of hers, they both looked at theirs and followed suit. She watched their facial expressions while they chewed the first bite. *It's like they've never eaten a peanut butter sandwich before. God, I hope neither one of them is allergic to peanuts*, she thought, briefly panicking. Very brief. On the other hand, that would be another very good reason to call 911. And more explainable.

"This is very good. Thank you." Joshua quickly ate the rest of the sandwich. He smiled when he saw Michael was enjoying his, a bit puzzled but enjoying it.

Michael turned to Joshua with a serious look. "We need to go back. You're not going to accomplish anything..." He paused. Gave Joshua a stern look. "...*else*...from down here. Azrael is –"

"I know. I stepped on his toes a bit this afternoon. I wasn't thinking, when I did it, brought her back," Joshua interrupted him.

"Are you talking about me?" she asked him.

Michael waved a hand at the girl, to silence her.

"Are you shushing me? In my own apartment?" Her eyes flashed a warning light, indignation rearing up. Un-fucking believable. *I've fed them. Can I still throw them out?* How does that work?

"We've got to follow the program. This is just a minor human nature thing. We'll figure it out. And Az is only concerned about you. We all are. We, *you* plus all of us, can accomplish more up... above," Michael tried to sound placating, and pointedly ignored the girl's outburst. He was relieved when she walked off into the living room and sank onto the couch.

Joshua's eyes followed her. She looked exhausted. "I'm staying here."

Joshua has that look in his eye, Michael thought. *And why are his eyes brown?*

"Look, you now know where to find me. Go up, calm everyone down. Bring Az down, if you must, but she stays here. He's not taking her now." Joshua watched the girl sink down into the couch, curl her feet up and lay her head down on a pillow. Hell of a day for her, he thought. When Michael's lack of response registered, he turned back to him. "What?"

"Do you *promise* to stay here?" Michael asked.

"I promise," he answered. "Well, as long as she

stays here. You know Az can track any of the souls, he'll be able to find me by looking for her."

The situation was so unusual Michael was at a loss how to proceed. He ran a frustrated hand through his hair, making it more of a mess than usual. He watched Joshua for a few moments. *He's fascinated with this soul,* he thought. Why? Was it because he just brought her back? Tampered with her timeline? He's right though, if he sticks with the girl, Az can find him. It's not like last time. "Fine. Fine!" He removed a small device from his back pocket and pointed it in the girl's direction, waited until it emitted a soft beep before putting it away. "I'm going up. You know Az won't be happy until he sees you, so expect him."

Joshua nodded to him, lost in his own thoughts. He caught Michael just before he simply dematerialized within the apartment, stopping him with a frantic hand gesture of caution. He mouthed, 'Use the door.' Before Michael closed it, he said, "Oh, and bring Christian down here... with the appropriate uplinks. We're going to need his predictive skills." He smiled when he watched Michael's shoulders rise and fall with an exaggerated sigh. Joshua laughed silently to himself. It's good to shake things up once in a while, he thought. Michael would get over it.

"You know he prefers the title Data Analyst, right?" Michael closed the door, not waiting for an answer.

When Joshua turned his attention back to the

girl, he found her sleeping. He took the knit blanket off the back of the couch and gently covered her. He watched her sleeping for a while. He was intrigued by the way humans could simply shut down, oblivious to their surroundings for hours at a time. He rarely slept, rarely had need of it. Plucking at his wet clothes in distaste, he snapped his fingers and they were replaced by dry blue jeans, black socks, black loafers, and a white button-down shirt. He ran his fingers through his wavy brown hair, trying to tame it to some semblance of order. He contemplated adjusting its length to something short and neat, more like Christian wore his, but he liked the way it felt brushing his shoulders. Long it stays, he thought.

He began wandering around her small apartment, curiosity led him to poke around. And poke his nose into things. He figured out the new style of plumbing in the watercloset. Perused the bedroom. The closet. Opened the cupboard doors in the kitchen, one at a time. He stood for some minutes in front of the open door of the refrigerator, contemplating its contents, or lack thereof. He finally settled in at the table in the kitchen and started reading papers she kept in files.

*****

John Stapleton arrived on the site, parked as close as he could, then joined the EMTs to assist if needed. There was a crowd of hushed on-lookers. He had to wade through them to reach the body. If you could still call it that. Jesus, he thought, can't be a single bone left intact. He looked up to the roof of the building. Another patrol car arrived, bringing more hands to move the crowd back.

John stepped aside. Reaching the curb, he gave into his stomach rebelling against what his eyes had just seen. He wiped his mouth, and blew out a deep breath, trying to steady himself. May have to rethink this volunteering shit, he thought. I'm calling in sick tomorrow. He looked at the ground at his feet. Good thing I forgot my coffee.

*****

Sitting at the kitchen table, Joshua shuddered. Another one. He drew a deep breath as he felt another soul separate from a body. That one was nearby, he thought. It's like they're accelerating. He breathed deep and waited for the dizziness to subside.

*****

Earth year 1918 CE, November 20th

Jenna Taylor awoke from a troubled sleep. The fever and coughing which had forced her to her cot in the nurse's barracks was gone. The barracks were mantled in heavy silence, a solitary lantern by the door was the sole source of illumination. The outline of a man suddenly appeared and began walking slowly toward her.

I must be dreaming, she thought, blinking. The door didn't open, did it? How could she not have heard it, and yet she was sure no one had been standing near it. She watched the man approach and recognized him as Death. She knew it was Death but didn't know how she knew. His were tired eyes, filled with sorrow, care-worn. Well, after four years of war, wouldn't Death be tired and worn out?

"I am Azrael, and I am here to collect you," he said. Simple, weighty, frightening words.

"Collect me?" Jenna asked. Startled, she rose from her cot.

"You're to be reassigned."

His voice was a deep rumble, resonating pleasantly, comfortable and warm. I could listen to that voice for hours, she thought. He should be on the radio. "I don't understand," she said, hoping to keep him talking, give her time to figure this out. Jenna knew the other nurses were concerned about her fever, but it felt like it had finally broken. She felt fine, but she definitely was not expecting visitors tonight. Let alone a tall, dark, and handsome man. Surreal.

Intrigued, she drew closer to him, reached out to touch him, confirm he was real.

"Come with me, child. It will be explained, and you will understand. Everything." He smiled encouragingly and beckoned with hand and voice. And deep brown eyes. "I will take you some place safe."

Together they dematerialized.

*****

A few hours passed before Michael returned to the apartment. He materialized just outside the apartment door, knocked softly and entered.

"Thought Azrael would be with you," Joshua said, looking up briefly from the file of paperwork he was reading. He kept his voice low, not wanting to disturb the girl now sleeping in the bedroom. After Michael left, he teleported her into the bedroom. *Handy being me,* he thought. *Sometimes.*

"Azrael's a little busy. These suicides." Michael shook his head. "I don't understand it."

"Neither do I. That's why I came down," Joshua said.

"Did you ask her why she did it?" Michael asked. Then frowning, asked, "Where is she, by the way?" He peered over the back of the couch where he had last seen her.

"I put her in the bedroom. She's exhausted," Joshua said. "I didn't get the chance to ask her. But I think I've discovered why." He pushed forward the file when Michael approached the kitchen table.

Michael opened it and began looking through it. "Past due, final notice, late fee applied. So, she's not good at managing her finances. That's no reason to –"

Joshua interrupted him. "Keep reading."

Michael got to the bill from the Shining Hope Nursing Home and frowned as he read it. "She's paying for her mother's care."

"Her grandmother, actually. Both her parents

are gone already." He placed another file on the table before Michael. It contained her bank statements and pay stubs. "She's working two jobs and can't make enough money to cover her grandmother's care, let alone to live on." He got up and opened cupboard doors, showing Michael they were empty except for coffee, the bread and the jar of peanut butter. "The refrigeration unit is basically empty as well. I wondered why she was so thin."

Michael slid down into a chair. "And she gave us her bread." Michael's voice was quiet, awed. *Be kind to strangers, and they will be kind to you.* He met Joshua's eyes. "We've got to figure out what is going wrong. Clearly, it's not human nature."

Joshua simply nodded. "We've got another glitch."

*****

She took a glass of red wine, her fourth, to the bathroom with her. The candles look so pretty burning next to the bathtub, she thought. She slid into the warm bath frothy with bubbles, downed the last of her glass. She picked up the razor blade lying on the edge of the tub and made precise cuts down her arms, neatly opening the veins on both wrists. She shook her long black hair over the edge of the tub and sank down for a comfortable soak. The wine eased her aching mind, the scent of the candles lured her away.

When her soul slipped its connection to her body, it waited in uncertainty.

*****

Michael watched Joshua waver slightly on his feet. When he heard him draw in a sharp breath, he knew. "Another one?"

Joshua turned a pale face to him, eyes bleak, and nodded slowly. He sank into the couch in the living room and lay his head against the back of it. "So near," he whispered.

Michael looked out the window, seeing flashing lights. Apparently very near.

THE THIRD DAY...

Sunday, July 5

Her alarm clock beside the bed showed 6:30. *AM or PM?* "God, what day is this?" she muttered to herself, shielding her eyes from the sun with her hands.

"I believe you call it Sunday. And it's morning."

That guy who calls himself God was sitting on the chair next to her bed. Normally the chair was piled high with clothes. She peeked between fingers to see a neat stack of folded clothes on top of her dresser. Crazy and a neat freak. The worst kind of crazy. When she looked at him, he smiled.

"You slept straight through the night," he said.

"Did you just sit there and watch me? Kind of creepy."

"No. Only checked on you. We've been working in the kitchen."

We? It registered then that there were other voices coming from her front room. More than just his friend, Michael, talking to himself. At least two other distinct voices.

"Who's we? And what do you mean working in my kitchen?"

"Just Michael, Azrael and my... I guess you would call him a data analyst." He smiled encouragingly, hoping to coax her out of the bedroom. "I was wondering..." He left off there, waiting, brows raised.

She waited for him to finish that thought. She was hoping this whole thing was a dream, one that would just go away, now that she was awake. Apparently, it wasn't going to. With a sigh, she sat up. "What? What were you wondering?"

He grinned. "There's this machine on your counter. I can't figure out what it is."

She got out of bed, pleased to find she was still clothed. Apartment full of crazy people, but at least none of them molested her while she slept. Thank God for small favors. *Wait. How did I get to the bedroom?* Shaking her head, must have been more tired than I thought. Small wonder.

In the kitchen, she added water to the Keurig, the machine in question, inserted a coffee pod, and placed a mug under the dispenser. Joshua watched her every move, fascination intense on his features. She looked at him, shaking her head, and pressed the Start button. "It's a Keurig. Coffee maker."

He looked at her with curiosity. And incomprehension.

"Oh, for the love of..." she muttered while extracting coffee-creamer from the fridge and more mugs from the cupboard. Systematically she filled and distributed mugs of coffee. When she sat down at her table, taken over by three men with computers and other strange devices, she looked at each in turn. She looked back at the crazy guy. *I can't call him God*, she thought. "Who are all of you and *what* are you doing in my apartment?"

Joshua sniffed the mug she handed him. He had watched her put white stuff in hers, so he added some to his, then took a tentative sip. "Coffee?" When she nodded, he said, "It's good." He looked at the other three, casually drinking their coffees. They've been down here often enough to have already tasted coffee. He wondered what else he'd been missing.

She cleared her throat, waiting for an answer to her question.

"I've already told you who I am," Joshua said. "And you've met Michael. This is Azrael," he said indicating the man with black hair, dark skin, and deep brown eyes.

Azrael nodded to her and held her eyes for a moment. She had that feeling, like they had met before, but she couldn't place it.

"And this," Joshua pointed to the young blond-haired man whose eyes were glued to the computer screen in front of him, "This is Christian. Our data analyst and tech geek."

Christian looked up at the sound of his name. "Oh, hello. You're awake."

She met his eyes briefly, blinked and shook her head. There was something...

Christian's eyes returned to the screen. "Ooh, this is a good thing!" he said with enthusiasm. "Look!" he said to Azrael.

Azrael nodded at what he saw on the screen. "Apparently, you were meant to bring her back," he said to Joshua.

His deep rich voice startled the girl. *I do know him, but from where? Voices, I always remember voices.* And eyes. She shook her head, trying to shake the feelings of déjà vu.

Watching the four men, listening to what they were saying, she began to feel lightheaded again. She set down her coffee mug and dropped her head into her hands. *This can't be really happening, can it?* she thought. *Breathe, just breathe. They think they are God and Archangels. Talking about some Program controlling Earth.*

Joshua approached her and gently lay his hand on her shoulder, emanating just a bit of his energy, willing her to look up at him. He waited patiently. He had caught the look of recognition on her face when she heard Azrael's voice. He knew she felt overwhelmed, but he needed her to accept the situation, the real facts. He did not yet understand what role she was about to play, but he knew she was necessary. The program might fuck up now and then, but his instinct had never failed him. When she finally met his eyes, he let them shift to green, to blue and back to brown. "Do you believe me now?" he asked quietly.

She could only nod. She swallowed a hard lump in her throat, sipped her coffee, and continued to watch things unfold in her kitchen.

"It will be okay, you'll see." Joshua looked deep into her eyes, trying his best to reassure her. He returned his attention to the others. "Christian, were you able to do what I asked?"

"Yep. Anonymous donors are easy to create. All taken care of," he said with only the briefest glance to Joshua.

"Show her." Joshua waited while Christian turned a screen towards the girl. He watched her face. A little frown creased her forehead as she made sense of what she was reading.

She raised her eyes first to Christian with disbelief and relief. Then she turned to... *I guess it's true...* she turned to God. "How? And... and why?"

He smiled and said, "I think you can guess *how*. And as to why? I need you. Alive." He felt better when he saw a smile curve her lips for the first time since they met.

*****

The yellow hard hat fluttered, caught in the updraft, taking its own sweet time to reach the ground. It came to land thirty odd feet from the body which had reached the ground in less than two seconds from an I-beam located seven stories up. The soul slipped up and away, rising higher in the sky. It hovered for a moment above the site, then faded, flickered, and was gone.

*****

"Ah!" Joshua gasped. He reached out to steady himself, closed his eyes and held his breath.

A small electronic device on the table near Azrael chimed. "Damn," he muttered when he read the small screen.

"Another one?" Christian asked, drawing back his hands which he instinctively had reached out in support toward Joshua. Seeing the glow emanating from him, he knew better than to touch him until it diminished.

"I'm sorry. We missed that one," Azrael said, looking concerned at the severity of Joshua's reaction to the soul now lost entirely. An impulsive leap from an apartment building being constructed in Ames, Iowa. No one had been available to collect the soul as it separated from the body.

*****

"Are you really telling me you've never been to a grocery store?" she asked. "Unfathomable."

Joshua flashed a grin at her. "Only a street market." He fished out of his shirt pocket a plastic card Christian had given him. "What is this? Christian didn't really explain it." They were walking down the street to the store, and now, she stopped just outside it, staring at him. He grinned. "Did I suddenly grow another head?"

She shook her head and reached for his card. On it she read Bank of Eternal Trust, VISA. Just a coded strip and chip. No numbers. No personal name. *Of course not.*

"You should put this in your wallet," she said, making to return it to him.

He looked at her with raised brows. "I don't have a wallet. Why don't you hold on to it?"

She looked down at the card again, before looking at him. "I am assuming while you are here, down here I mean, you all need to eat like… the rest of us?" She slipped the card into the back pocket of her jeans.

His stomach growled in answer. He raised his eyebrows at her. "Let's food shop. And later, maybe we can go over to that shopping mall and look around. I've never been in one of those either."

She blinked, several times.

Okay, groceries it is.

I wonder where they're all going to sleep.

Is it too late to call 911?

No way to explain this.

Not without sounding crazy.

She inclined her head toward the sliding doors to the store entrance, and they began his first experience 'food shopping.' They wandered up and down aisles, stopping frequently. Joshua kept picking things up, studying them, smelling some. When he tried to taste a pear, she stopped him.

"You have to pay for it first." She picked

out several pears, apples, and a bunch of bananas from the available fruits. The cart looked like she planned to feed an army.

"It's really unfair the others get to come down here more often than I do. They're familiar with all this. Things have changed so much." He waved his hand around them. "There's so much more... Of everything."

"When was the last time you were... here?" she asked.

He mumbled a number and looked away. She grabbed his arm and made him look her in the eye. He sighed and said, "1918." He watched her blink, several times.

"And how long have you been coming down... here?" Her eyes were wide open, breaths coming in shallow gasps.

He held her elbow, afraid she might fall to the floor. "More than 2000 years. Earth years, that is."

She blinked, more than a few times. Again. "So much for immaculate conception then, huh?"

He rolled his eyes, avoiding hers.

"Buddy, you've got some serious explaining to do."

"Why do you call me Buddy?" He tilted his head and looked at her with a slight crease in his brow.

"I can't very well go around calling you God," she said in a whisper. "People will think we're crazy." She slapped a hand to her forehead. "I cannot believe I'm having this conversation."

*****

Schenectady, New York: The Daily Gazette – Local News

Fatal Collision takes life of local man. Arthur Madsen, age 47, was found dead on the scene. The vehicle he was driving veered from the roadway and crashed into a utility pole in the northbound ditch. Time of crash estimated between 1:00 AM and 3:00 AM when the crash was sighted by local law enforcement officer. Madsen was last seen leaving the Centre Street Public House establishment around 12:30 AM.

Local couple found dead in their garage. Carbon monoxide poisoning suspected, no foul-play suspected. Names withheld pending notification of next of kin.

*****

Portland, Oregon: The Willamette Week – Local News

4 Dead in what investigators believe to be a murder/suicide in the 200 block Couch St, near Old Town, Saturday night. This is an on-going homicide investigation; no further details are available at time of print.

*****

Back at the apartment, Julia began preparing spaghetti sauce. The old-fashioned way. No jarred sauce ever graced her family's table, and she wasn't about to cheat now. Not with these guests. Five to cook for, she thought. I haven't had this many to feed since Dad passed away. While she cooked, the others worked around her kitchen table. Cooking gave her something to think about, and she needed a distraction. A major distraction. Over the next couple of hours, she tried not to pay attention to her host of angelic guests. Completely, utterly weird. More than once, she raised her eyes heavenward and wondered if her dad was watching.

"Christian, you're going to have to move all that," she said, indicating the computers and other devices. "Dinner's almost ready." She finished slicing the loaf of sourdough bread, thinking how wonderful it was to use someone else's credit card. She set the bread basket and butter on the table.

When Azrael offered to help, she handed him napkins and silverware to distribute. She then began filling plates with pasta and sauce, handing them one at a time to Azrael. Her mouth watered at the aroma. Everyone else was breathing it in deeply as well. For a change they were all quiet. *Don't look closely*, she thought, *their tails might be wagging.*

Once seated, she cast her eyes around the table. This is just really as weird as it can get, she thought. I'm sitting down to dinner with God, two of archangels, and she looked at Christian, unsure of his designation. *Do we pray?* Her eyes rested on God and thought, thanks would be very appropriate in this particular case. At that precise moment, he met her eyes and smiled. *I think he can read my thoughts.*

Very well then. Thank you, she thought and smiled at him.

"Would you pass the bread, please?" he asked. *She's quick on the uptake, I'll give her that.* And he was impressed she hadn't freaked out. Yet. He studied the technique she was using to eat the spaghetti. Twirl the fork. The first taste brought a look of absolute delight to his face and kicked his taste buds into overdrive.

"Do you like it?" she asked, all the while knowing the answer. He only nodded as his mouth was full. She smiled. "It's my dad's recipe. He was a fantastic cook. Good thing, 'cause my mother hated cooking." Her voice trailed off. Thinking about her father always made her sad.

"What's wrong," Joshua asked, keeping his voice low so only she heard him.

She just shook her head. "It's nothing."

"Whatever it is, it's made you sad."

She was grateful when he didn't pursue it. "Oh, my apologies, everyone. I forgot the wine." When she made to rise to get it, Michael stopped her.

"Please, allow me." Michael picked up the bottle from the counter, read the label – Pinot Noir. He coaxed the cork out and poured five glasses. He swirled his first sip around his tongue. "Not bad, girl. You know your wine."

She smiled, and silently thanked her father.

Her attention was drawn back to God when she heard his sharp intake of breath. Without a thought, she lay her hand on his arm, concern etched in the wrinkle of her brow.

With her hand on his arm, Joshua had to concentrate on keeping his energy level low. It served as a distraction from the pain he absorbed. He rode through it, willing it to subside.

Azrael checked his small device at its chime. "I'll be back," he said. He stepped into the hallway and dematerialized.

*****

Azrael materialized in the alleyway behind the Shell Station in Roselt, Texas. The soul was hovering above the body of the teenaged girl. She was leaning against the outer wall of the convenience store, concealed by an old rusty dumpster and the smell of garbage. Azrael's shoulders slumped at the sight of the hypodermic in the dead girl's hand. He held out his open hand to the soul trembling beside him, "Come child, I will take you some place safe." The energy and light drifted close and then enveloped his hand and arm. At its touch, Azrael dematerialized.

*****

Joshua became very quiet. He ate slowly. A distant look in his eyes indicated his withdrawal from the present location. The atmosphere became subdued, everyone ate in silence, casting occasional glances toward Joshua. Julia stared hard at Christian until he met her inquiring eyes. He shook his head, letting her know there was nothing anyone else could do. They did not have to wait for Azrael's return to know he was successful in this retrieval.

Joshua gave a shake of his head, breathed deep and looked around the table, finally noticing the quiet which had settled in. "More wine, anyone?" he asked, trying to find some sense of normal.

Azrael returned, and with a nod toward Joshua, resumed his meal.

Later Julia was quietly washing dishes and putting food away, lost in thought. Trying not to freak out. Again. The others had returned to their discussion of numbers, suicide rates and projections. She suspected they were speaking in code to exclude her. She didn't care. It was still so surreal, she found she didn't mind not knowing exactly what they were working on. She was pulled from her thoughts when she noticed God standing next to her with a dishtowel in hand.

"I'll dry," Joshua said, taking a wineglass from her hand. He did not like how quiet she had become since dinner. The others were excluding her from their discussion. He didn't agree it was necessary. In fact, he'd rather the opposite was happening. He wanted her in on the discussion. Who better to ask how to fix this mess than someone who lived here on Earth, every day? One who had already tried to end her life. Not just tried, he amended. He wanted her insight on the mess they'd allowed to happen.

"If you like." She smiled as she watched him, noticing he seemed pretty familiar with where things were to be stored in her cupboards. "Did more than a little snooping while I was sleeping, didn't you?" She raised an eyebrow at him.

He gave her a shy, and somewhat sheepish, look. "Sorry."

"I think I can forgive you." It was her turn to feel shy and sheepish. She had yet to thank him for what he had done for Gran's nursing home bill. She watched him dry the last of the silverware and place it in the tray in the drawer. "I don't know how I can ever –"

He stopped her with a finger to her lips. "It was the least I could do." He didn't remove his finger until he was sure she wouldn't renew her efforts to thank him. After all she'd been through in this one life alone. So much suffering, so little joy. And this was only one of the billions of souls on Earth today. Guilt was weighing heavy enough on him. Her thanks would only have added to the burden. At her nod, he removed his finger from across her lips. He hung up the towel and took her hand. He led her back to the table and said to the others, "All right. It's time. I want her fully briefed."

Christian's hands froze on his virtual keyboard, his mouth hung open.

Michael gasped and was about to object.

Azrael silenced Michael with a hand on his arm. "Excellent decision. But where do we begin?"

Joshua looked at the girl with a grin. "I think she knows the beginning, so how about we start with the problem at hand and what it is we do." He held a chair out for her to sit. "More wine, anyone?" He chuckled when all their glasses were pushed toward him.

Azrael's device chimed again.

Joshua stifled a groan. "Send someone else, Az. I want you here."

Azrael nodded and tapped a command into the device.

*****

Dressed in the black clothing Azrael insisted his assistants wear, the guardian materialized in the bedroom of the Manhattan flat. Music played softly from the device on the table next to the bed. A handsome man of forty or so years appeared to be sleeping. The guardian knew he wasn't. The soul hovered near the ceiling directly above the bed, calmly pulsing, waiting.

"Come along, little one. It's all right, now," the guardian said as she gestured with her hand for it to come to her. "I will take care of you." When it alighted on to her shoulder, she said, "There, now. Off we go." The room plunged into sudden darkness at their departure.

*****

The group gathered in Julia's apartment moved to seats in the living room.

"Wait, what happens in times of war? You really try to retrieve all the souls of the fallen?" Julia's mind grappled with the numbers. The dead, the number of assistants Azrael would have needed for WWI, WWII, Korea, Vietnam, the Gulf War. Roman legions conquering Europe and beyond. Her mind whirled with just these which quickly came to mind. She shook her head, unable to fathom the work involved. "And epidemics like the Black Death, cholera, small pox?"

"Yes, we try to retrieve them all. There's a finite number of souls. We don't want to lose a single one if we can help it." Azrael answered and then shot a stern look at Joshua when he saw he was about to interject. There was an exception to that rule, a method to create new souls, but Azrael did not feel this was the time to make her aware of it.

"Surely, you miss some now and then. So, the number of people here on Earth should be depleting, not increasing," Julia said, looking as confused as she felt.

Azrael waited for her to meet his eyes before he answered her. "There are a lot of souls residing in what you call heaven and on other planets. We shift them around trying to maintain a balance, and yet not exceed the maximum sustainability on each planet. Earth has not reached its maximum capacity. But it is quickly approaching it." He watched her carefully while she processed that. *She has interesting facial expressions when she's thinking,* he thought. He smiled, a rare commodity for him. He was amused by her, something he hadn't experienced in nearly a century. *Joshua is fascinated with her too,* he thought. *Again.* He sighed inwardly. *Deal with that later, if we must,* he thought. "What is it? It's natural you should have questions."

Her brow remained creased as she formed her thoughts into a question. "These other planets. Do the souls who live there, look like us. Humans, I mean?"

"Some. Not all."

"Are the souls interchangeable then? From one planet to another?"

He hesitated and covered it by taking a sip of wine, glancing at Michael who nodded for him to continue. "Child, souls are more like energy and light, a sentient essence. Does that help you to understand?"

Julia nodded, but remained silent, contemplative.

Joshua watched her intently, still waiting for her to freak out. They'd been through this, countless times in the past and usually didn't get this far before ending the briefing with a memory wipe.

"So, when someone here dies, you collect their soul and take them –?"

"To heaven, as you call it."

"Does your..." she waved her hand at Christian's computers, "Program determine the length of every lifespan or are they random?" She was thinking of her parents, both gone by the time she turned twenty-five.

"Most souls are allowed to live as long as they choose or at least as long as the body they inhabit can maintain their presence. Others are predetermined." Azrael was worried where this line of questioning could go. He noticed Christian biting his lip, and Michael looked like he had forgotten to breathe. Under the coffee table he lightly kicked Michael's foot, startling him enough to realize he was looking a bit too tense.

"What if all the souls did not want to leave heaven, not return to the planets? Can heaven sustain them all?" she asked.

Azrael brows shot up. He was not expecting that question. He looked to the others for help. Surprise registered on all their faces. Usually this is where the human asks why someone in their life died young.

Christian cleared his throat, and raised his eyebrows, questioning Joshua if he could answer her. At his nod, he said, "Up until recently, most souls wanted to be experiencing life on a planet."

"Is Earth the only planet experiencing this rash of suicides?" she asked, looking at Christian. He was their data analyst after all.

Christian nodded. "Just Earth." He could almost see the wheels of her mind going at high speed behind her brown eyes. "What are you thinking?" Joshua wanted her briefed for whatever reason of his own, but Christian intended to pick her brain for as much information as he could get. It was a fair exchange.

"I think Earth has already reached its maximum capacity, as you call it." Her eyes ran around the room to all of theirs in turn. "I don't mean we're running out of food. Let me try to explain." She momentarily rested her forehead on her fingertips, elbows propped on her drawn up knees. She blew out a deep breath, tried to organize her thoughts and, she admitted to herself, dredge up the courage to explain why she attempted to end her own life. "Lack of money was not my only reason." She looked up then and continued without being able to make eye contact directly with any of them. They were formidable in their silence, and she was feeling rather small in her own home. She waved her hand around her shabby apartment, and said, "This isn't how I imagined my life would turn out. I don't mean I expected wealth and a huge house, that sort of thing. What I really mean is, I hate living in the city with so many people around me. I feel claustrophobic, panicky. I *had* to come here to find work. This apartment is all I can afford here in town. But what would really make me happy, content, would be a small cabin up north, in the woods, with the nearest neighbor miles away. A small family with a simple life."

"A simple life," Christian repeated. He smiled at her. "Like a Hobbit?"

She smiled, shook her head, not surprised to find him well-versed in Earth literature. "Not exactly. Just not this rat-race." She looked around the table, met by blank faces. "I don't think I'm the only one who feels there are just too many people on Earth. It gets harder and harder to get away from them all, to get a break, time out. Solitude. There's no space, no room to breathe. Everybody fighting, hating each other." She watched them all exchanging glances and wondered if they didn't have some form of telepathic communication going on between them. She couldn't tell for certain. "I think all the political crap - the racism, religious intolerance, isolationist attitude, discrimination based on gender or sexuality – all of that is just… like a symptom. A picture of what we're facing now. Too many people rubbing elbows, egos collide, kill the one that isn't like us mentality. Too many in too small of a space."

"So, you're saying there's a psychological threshold. Sustainability being more than enough food and shelter?" Christian looked at her with serious interest.

"Psychological, or more precisely, an aesthetic threshold," she said, pleased Christian was getting her point. "There's no place to wander anymore. We can't all just exist like sardines in a can. Piled on top of one another." She gestured with her hand to indicate her apartment building. "There's too much fight in our nature."

Azrael leaned back in his chair, nodding. "Some of the first peoples of Earth were hunters and gatherers, basically living nomadic lifestyles. Scattered small groupings which only fought when one group infringed on the territory of another."

"Precisely," she said. "We can't forget there are many who just need solitude. The wanderers. The lone poet. I don't think we were meant to… become so numerous." Her voice trailed off softly as her own words echoed through the room.

Christian looked especially thoughtful. "Maybe these suicides, these souls are those who have foreseen what is to come and either can't abide it, or..." He stopped and looked at Julia, worried by the look on her face, the blank stare in her eyes. "Or they are selfless enough to remove themselves from existence to set others free. Sacrificing themselves for the good of others... not selfish acts of defiance... or sad failures to adapt."

"Like me," Julia said softly. She hated her life. She'd given up. A failure.

"No." Joshua interrupted her thoughts. "You were carrying more on your shoulders than you were meant to."

Michael and Azrael exchanged a look at Joshua's quick defense of the girl.

"We need to figure out a course of action," Michael said. "Suggestions?"

Christian looked at Joshua. "I think we need to bring Gabriel and Ariel down here."

"And perhaps, Chamuel," Joshua said. "It'll leave Raphael and Uriel a bit short-handed."

"I'll go," Michael said. "I can stay and give them a hand until you need me."

"Az, my monitor's been going crazy while we've been talking. You're needed up above as well," Christian said. "They're swamped." He shot a quick look at Joshua, having noticed his degree of quietude increased in direct correlation with the numbers on his screen, the number of souls exiting Earth. He knew Joshua felt them. Every. Single. One.

Michael and Azrael left through the door. Joshua knew they would dematerialize as soon as the door closed. No need to freak the girl out any more than we already have, he thought. He watched her for a minute trying to gauge her reaction to what she had been told. "Are you all right?"

She nodded. "What kind of suggestions is Michael looking for?"

Joshua suddenly wanted to look anywhere except in her eyes, yet he forced himself to maintain eye contact. "We need Gabriel and his assistants to talk a few of these suicidal souls off ledges, or bridges." Julia gave him an 'Oh, please' look. "And Ariel can give us a new idea of a sustainable population estimate. What it's going to take to give people room to breathe, as you said."

"So, all that does happens, here on Earth, you don't really interfere? Unless too many souls are being lost?" Her idea of the role of God was being forced to shift significantly. Along with her whole fucking concept of reality.

"Right. All the politics, economics, social affairs – that's all human nature, how the species has evolved." Joshua threw his hands up and shook his head, reminded of past failures to steer human society. In the end, it hadn't done a damn bit of good.

"We create the problems, so we should be the ones to fix them," she said.

"I can't interfere," Joshua agreed.

"Well, we could –" Christian jumped in.

"Chris, I said no," Joshua interrupted him.

"But –"

"Chris, you'll understand. One day." Joshua gave him the 'Shut Up' look. Discussion closed. But only for now, knowing Christian.

"But right now. You're saying this is a problem we can't fix on our own." She frowned and then turned her eyes to God. "Now what?"

"All signs are pointing to you being correct. That Earth is overpopulated. Either we let the suicides continue, losing countless souls, or this time we must intervene to save the souls."

"But not to save lives." Julia said, barely audible. "Are you saying Earth needs another war? Or Plague?" *Christ, what a horrible idea.*

"It needs to be an historical event that makes sense, something explainable," Joshua said. "Apparently, my wrath upon the world doesn't carry as much weight as it once did."

"A virus would be easiest. Quickest." Christian had already been exploring this option. "We can program a quick acting virus that mutates to a non-fatal form after thirty-six hours."

Julia went quiet, the color drained from her face. "Is there no other choice?"

Joshua reached for her hand and held it between his own. *Screaming should start any time now.* "We won't act before we explore all the options. The big picture, that's our focus."

She surprised him with a relatively calm

voice. "What happens if a soul does not want to leave its body? Doesn't want to die? Do they have a choice?" She was looking at Christian when she spoke and saw him freeze with a look of panic on his face. She turned to God for an answer. She held his gaze, unflinching.

"If it's necessary, we take them anyway." Joshua spoke softly and tried to hold her eyes with his, but she looked away, inward. He hated this part of any briefing they attempted. When a soul doesn't consent, a flame of betrayal is lit, and the soul begins its diminishing. He didn't want this one to diminish.

"I'm going for a walk." She abruptly pulled her hand free, grabbed her jean jacket and walked out of the apartment.

Joshua sat looking at the door, stunned by her abrupt departure. *She walked out on me!*

"Aren't you going after her?" Christian asked. "With all she knows, not good to have her out walking about."

"I'd better, hadn't I? She might try it again." Joshua dematerialized and reappeared outside the apartment, looking hastily around for any trace of her. He spotted her heading in the direction of the river. She was walking slow, hands tucked in the pockets of her jacket, head down. He followed but didn't try to catch up, wanting to see where she went, knowing she was lost in thought. He was wavering between betting on the bridge or the path along the river. She veered left once she was clear of the shopping mall parking lot. "Bridge it is," he said to himself, and hurried his steps.

She stopped halfway across, the same as the other day, but did not climb over the guardrail. She leaned her legs against it, just stood looking out over the burbling waters below. He approached silently and stood a few feet away, just watching her. Ready to grab her if necessary. After a while, he was convinced she was not going to jump. There'd been no hesitation the other day.

"Should I jump in, so you can save me again?" He saw that brought a smile to her face. When she turned to him, he tried his best to look innocent, and pantomimed diving.

She just rolled her eyes at him. "I really don't feel like getting wet, so please don't." She remained still while he came closer. "How is it in all the years you've lived... existed... you never learned to swim?"

"Not sure. The others get to spend more time on the planets than I do. When I do come down, I'm usually a bit preoccupied." He turned and leaned back on the guardrail, so he could face her. He wanted to watch her expression. The sun warmed her brown eyes to the color of caramels. He remembered liking caramels. "Why haven't you freaked out about all this?" He kept his voice quiet and soothing. "We rarely get this far when explaining things."

"Oh, trust me, I'm freaking out. I'm just doing it silently," she said. "Are you really over two thousand years old?"

He nodded. Two thousand and twenty, he thought.

"And you're not the original God, who created Earth as we see it."

Again, he nodded. "Correct. There were several before me."

"So, you must have a name. Besides God."

He was silent for a few minutes, wondering what to say. They all assumed their titles as their names when they took their positions. I don't even remember Michael's original name, and I've known him the longest, he thought. He drew a deep breath and let it out slowly. *Oh, what the hell.* "I've come to Earth under many names. But originally, my name was Joshua."

"Joshua." She said it softly, blurring the middle consonant blend. "I like that."

And he liked the sound of it, in her voice, formed by her mouth. His eyes focused on her mouth, then travelled downward. Earth was waking up more than just his stomach and taste buds. Listening to her, watching her. He shook his head. He had forgotten this effect. Or tried to forget it.

"Have you ever tasted ice cream, Joshua?" She smiled when he frowned at the abrupt subject change.

He shook his head slowly. "Not that I recall."

She indicated with her head they should start walking back toward the mall. "Come on. You're going to try Dairy Queen. Grandpa always said ice cream was good for the soul."

*****

Joshua watched while she ordered two small ice cream concoctions, and he peered through the window while they were prepared. She was laughing silently at him when he looked back at her.

"This will be one of many bad habits I could teach you," she said as she watched him taste his first spoonful. She dipped her spoon into hers.

"Wow." He shut his eyes, savoring Cookies N Cream. "First, your dad's special recipe spaghetti sauce and now this."

They sat down at a bench outside and ate silently. Well, almost silently. He kept emitting sounds of delighted rapture while she laughed at him.

She looked around, making sure no one could overhear their conversation. "How many lifetimes have I lived?"

He finished the last bite of his ice cream before he answered. "I don't know. Christian could find that answer." He made finger movements like tapping on a keyboard. Then he tilted his head and asked, "Why?"

"Just curious," she said as she scraped the last of the ice cream from the paper cup. "Sometimes, I just feel like I've been around forever. We call it, an old soul. Does that make sense?"

He nodded. Quietly, he said, "You recognized Azrael." He had sensed it when she first met him.

"His voice," she whispered. "And his eyes."

"It happens. You're not the first." He had a few questions to pose for Christian, too. He was curious why both of her parents were gone so young. Why she was on her own at twenty-seven. Earth years. Blink of an eye, from his perspective.

"Penny for your thoughts," she said.

"Let's talk to Christian when we get back." He took the cup from her hand and deposited both in a trash receptacle. He offered her a hand up, "Ready?"

She nodded and accepted his hand.

*****

They walked back to the apartment and found Christian still with his eyes glued to multiple monitors and screens. She noticed the number of screens had increased by four, at least. "We probably shouldn't mention the ice cream," she whispered.

"Ah, you're back. No midnight swim then, I take it?" Christian smiled at them.

"Ha. Ha. Is it that late?" she asked. "I'd better get to bed. I work in the morning." She caught the slight look of concern on both their faces. "What?"

"Well, um..." Christian stopped. He turned to Joshua. "You tell her."

Joshua shot him an acidic look. He gave her a slightly apologetic look. "You don't really have a job anymore."

"I think you'd better explain," she said, sitting on the arm of the couch. "How did I manage to lose my job?"

"He did it." Joshua pointed at Christian.

"It was your idea!"

"Was not."

"It was his idea. He didn't want you out of his sight, so he asked me to put money in your bank account to take care of your bills. And send a letter of resignation to the clinic." Christian grinned at her. "So, you don't have to work tomorrow. That's a good thing, right?"

"Did you ever think to ask if I wanted you to do that? I mean, I'm grateful for your help with my grandmother's nursing home bill, but what am I going to do after you all leave? I need that job." She looked from one to the other.

Christian looked back and forth between Julia and Joshua, and finally pointed both forefingers at Joshua. "Ball's in your court, old man."

Joshua slowly raised his eyes to meet hers, and found her frozen, all the color drained from her face. "You'll get a fresh start," he said. She started to shake her head, and tremble. She looked like she was going to...

He caught her before she hit the floor and carried her to the bedroom. He tucked her in and took a seat on the chair beside the bed.

Christian yelled from the kitchen table. "It's really amazing she lasted this long!"

Joshua dragged his fingers through his hair. This was getting way more complicated than he thought it would. Michael was always yelling at him for doing things without thinking them through.

What have I done? If I hadn't come down here, she'd already be in Azrael's hands. She could have been into a new timeline or hung out in heaven for a while. She was ready. But now... now, she wasn't. Now, she wanted to stay. Julia Altieri wanted to live.

*****

Earth year 1640

Twenty-two years of conflict in the Holy Roman Empire. Over seven million deaths. Soldiers dying in battle, collateral deaths of innocents. Men, women, children. Soul after soul needing to be collected, comforted and reassigned. Joshua watched the monitors and grew angry.

"Michael, this can't go on!" he said. "They are killing one another over words. Distorted words, at that." Every death the souls felt, he felt. This had to stop soon. He wasn't sure how much more he could bear.

Michael watched the muscles in Joshua's jaw quiver, knowing there was a battle raging as they spoke. Azrael was more or less encamped down on earth, a base set up in central Europe. "You want to go down, don't you?"

Joshua turned bleak eyes to him and nodded. "I think I'd better. I'll take Raphael and Gabriel with me. We must find a way to make these pigheaded factions talk and stop killing each other."

"Do you mean to show yourself? In your true form, I mean." Michael held his breath. The wrath of God had been extremely useful in the past, especially where these stubborn humans were concerned. Lately though, Joshua had been hesitant to blatantly force change, as well as reveal himself.

"No, Micha, my friend, I don't believe more violence is needed. We need to encourage peace, not the opposite." Joshua stopped, ran a hand through his already mussed up hair. The more frustrated he felt, the more disheveled his hair became. "My original message… lost in the winds of time."

"So, whispers in the appropriate ears, then?" Michael asked.

"Yes, and it won't be easy. This could take a while." Joshua looked back to the screen in front of him, the one depicting a map of the territories under disputes. "I know you won't let me out of your sight," he said, effectively stalling a forthcoming objection he sensed in Michael. "I suggest you and I base in Munster. Raphael and Gabe in Osnabruck."

"I'll inform them. When do you want to go down?" Michael asked as he was heading out through The Office door.

"The sooner, the better," Joshua said.

Munster

The great hall was wall to wall with trestle tables laden with food and drink. The gathered nobles and their retainers ate, drank, shouted, belched, farted, argued and were not getting any closer to finding a consensus of thought regarding a division of European territories.

Joshua and Michael exchanged looks from across the room. A word here, a word there. One word at a time, pushing for peace. Joshua felt like a shepherd to a pack of snarling bitches. Or a herd of stallions in need of gelding. If Father only knew what my teaching had been perverted into, he thought, shaking his head. Where did we fail? He'd been trying to curb the religious zealots for hundreds of years and felt like he continuously waded in horseshit. Still, we have delegates from most of the conflicted nations here, so that was a start. He looked away briefly from a conversation with the man seated next to him. A serving girl was filling his cup.

"Thank you." He nodded once to her when she raised her eyes to his. Uncommonly pretty, he thought. Light brown hair tied back and falling to her slim waist, soft brown eyes, fresh skin. He smiled as he watched her move down the table, filling other glasses. He was still watching and smiling when she looked back to him. A slight blush rose on her cheeks before she turned away. His attention was reclaimed by the man beside him. Back to work, he thought. No time for anything else. Still, he could not stop his eyes seeking the girl's form throughout the evening.

Hours passed, and the meal dragged on. The more wine that flowed, the louder the gathered nobles talked. Excusing himself for the evening, in desperate need to empty his near bursting bladder,

Joshua slipped out of the hall. He knew Michael would stick it out long into the night, but he'd reached his limit. His head ached. He circled his arms above him and flexed his shoulders with a groan. Somewhere out there, people were still slaughtering each other. He could feel it, every last bloody one of them. And it was beginning to wear him down. He spied a dark, out of the way spot where he could at last relieve himself. Before stepping into the shadows, he looked around to make sure he would not be disturbed. Nearly finishing the process, his ears picked up sounds of a struggle.

He cast about trying to see the cause and heard a muffled feminine scream and the sound a hand makes when it suddenly connects with flesh. Sounds which told him a woman was being assaulted. Where?

He rushed into the shadows of the nearby stables. The sound of struggling grew louder until he came upon a man holding a girl by her hair pressed up against the wall of the stable and fumbling to lift her skirts up from behind. Joshua's eyes flashed and without even a hint of hesitation, a force pulsed from him separating the man from the girl. The man flew into the stonewall, his head making a sickening thud, and he collapsed into stillness.

The girl, suddenly free from her assailant, fell to the ground. She got up and looked around wildly, trying to figure out how she was suddenly free. Her hair free from its ties fell across her face. She pushed it aside and gasped at the sight of the man standing near her. He glowed, pulsing like a furious lightning strike. Another bright orb of pulsating light was drawn toward him, into him, staggering the man slightly. She gasped.

Joshua turned at the sound the girl made. "You," he said. It was the serving girl. "Are you all right?"

She nodded. Her eyes still wide with fright.

"It's all right. I'm not going to hurt you." He spoke softly and slowly approached her. He quelled the light emanating from him, and darkness returned to the stable now lit only by the feeble light of stars and a waning moon. He reached out with a slow hand to gently touch her tear streaked cheek. When she cringed with a sob, he said, "You're safe now. What is your name?"

"Joella," she said, just before she collapsed, senseless.

He gathered her up in his arms. "Now, what do I do with you?" He carried her back to the apartments he was assigned within the castle. The serving women will sort this out.

Joella Renati, at seventeen years of age, awoke hours later knowing she had looked into the eyes of God. She kept what she had witnessed to herself but was determined to thank him for rescuing her. She waited and watched and at last found him walking amongst the pear trees in the orchard, alone but for the one companion who usually kept company with him. She approached, swallowed her fear, and knelt before him.

"What is this?" Michael asked, turning to Joshua.

She wasn't sure just how she should address him, but with lowered eyes and great respect, she proceeded. "My lord, I wish to thank you, for rescuing me last night." Joella's voice quavered but was clear.

Michael raised his eyebrows.

Joshua waved him off. He reached down to assist the girl to her feet. "I am pleased you did not come to more harm." She wouldn't look him in the face, trembled at his touch. "Joella?" He waited until she raised her eyes to his. "You need never fear me."

He was struck by an odd feeling when their eyes met. Like the night before, he was drawn to her. He wanted to pull her close, hold her, protect her. And kiss those trembling lips.

She came willingly to him. Hesitantly, she lifted her hand to his cheek, and with a mutual sigh, an understanding was reached, lingering deep.

The memory of Joella stayed with Joshua long after the Treaty of Westphalia was signed.

THE FOURTH DAY...

Monday July 6

The following morning, Christian was again working at the kitchen table. Joshua watched the monitors and screens. Christian had them scrolling so fast they were almost a blur. He tapped one to slow it, fighting vertigo. The number of suicides still escalated. Written plain as day on the screen. And written within his own soul. Julia was right, there were more occurring in the metropolitan areas, in fact four times as many.

"Chris, how do you look at all these screens at this speed?" he asked, shaking his head. "She was right, you know?"

"Higher numbers in the cities?" Christian nodded, and returned to his screens. "I've been trying to generate a comparison of the production in the arts, now versus ten years ago, and think I've got enough data. Everything is up – music, painting, writing, dance. You name it, the arts have exploded. Generally, you see this when the economy is booming, and people have more free time on their hands. But that's not the case, so there's got to be another explanation." He handed a tablet to Joshua. "Take a look at this. Scroll through for a while, and then tell me what you think."

Joshua's brow furled while scrolling. "This all is so... dark."

Christian only nodded.

"Julia?" Joshua looked around for her. "Where is she?"

Christian shook his head. "Thought you were keeping an eye on her."

They were both relieved when she came through the apartment door a moment later. Carrying a basket of clothes, she headed down the short hallway toward the bedroom. Joshua followed her, curious.

"Where were you?" he asked.

"Laundry room." She smiled when she saw confusion on his face. "Washing clothes." She pointed to the basket, and then started putting the clean clothes into drawers and hanging some in the tiny closet.

He just stood near the door and watched her go through this almost ritual-like behavior. Interesting, he thought, wash clothes to reuse them. He looked down at what he was wearing. Jeans, white cotton button-down shirt. He changed clothes daily with a snap of his fingers. Looking at her varied wardrobe, he wondered if he should put on a different colored shirt. Maybe light blue, and he snapped his fingers. He looked up to find her staring at him. "Oops."

"I was wondering how you managed to get the spaghetti stain out of your white shirt. Now, I know."

He grinned. "You're not going to faint again, are you?"

She shook her head, smiling. *What an imp.*

"Could you come into the kitchen? I'd like you to look at something." He waited for her to pass through the doorway and precede him down the hall. "Here, this screen. Scroll through."

She picked up the screen and sat on the couch in the living room. Scrolling, she wasn't sure *what* exactly she was looking at. Movie posters, play billboards, song lyrics, art exhibits, poetry, book covers. "This all looks so gloomy, almost depressing," she said. "What is all this?"

"The latest artistic output from New York, Paris, Tokyo, London, Mumbai and Rio," Christian answered her without looking up. "Just a sampling, but you nailed the consistency. That and the fact that more suicides are happening in the larger cities. Got any other insights you want to share?"

"Is the rate higher in the U.S.?"

Christian changed monitors, tapped a few keys. "Huh." He looked at her, impressed. "Now, why would you say that?"

"Seriously? Have you not paid attention to

our latest political situation?" Julia asked. "You are lucky half the population of the U.S. isn't knockin' on heaven's door."

Christian and Joshua exchanged a look. Again, causing her to think there was some form of silent communication going on between the two of them.

"I'm on it," Christian said, and returned to his monitors.

*****

Promontory Drive, Bismarck, North Dakota. A fire as bright as the sun blazed in spite of the efforts of the firemen and trucks at the front of the house. Azrael and one of his assistant guardians arrived on the edge of the woods surrounding the house. They waited, looking in vain for the seven souls which were seemingly lost in the housefire.

*****

As Joshua returned the screen to Christian, he drew in a sharp breath, stumbled and fell into one of the kitchen chairs. His face lost all color, and his breath came in short gasps. Eyes closed, he waited for it to pass.

"Josh!" Julia flew off the couch and was at his side in an instant.

He clutched her hand, unable to speak or even open his eyes. Christian watched in amazement. Joshua was glowing pretty hot, yet Julia didn't appear to feel it. He was further amazed

Joshua didn't quell the energy at contact, instead he leaned into Julia, and she put her other arm around him as well.

"Seven at once, completely lost," Julia said.

"What?" Christian was astonished.

"He said seven were lost." She looked at Christian, tilted her head in question. "What?"

"He didn't say anything... aloud," Christian said. *Holy hell, she heard his thoughts.*

Julia froze, then looked down to Joshua who was only just then trying to open his eyes and take some normal breaths. She looked back to Christian. "What the hell just happened here?"

Christian shook his head and mouthed, '*no idea*'.

*****

She made sandwiches for lunch and placed one near everyone's elbow while they continued to work. Azrael had just arrived and was now resting his eyes in the living room. He jumped when she touched his shoulder and offered him a plate. He's the only one she'd seen rest. But then, that was only natural. Angel of Death, and all. Lot of soul-guiding happening, that was what he called it.

"Thank you." He examined the sandwich. "Peanut butter again?"

"Ha, ha. Ham and cheese." She sat down on the other end of the couch and began eating. "Can I ask you something?" She smiled when a worried look crossed his face. When he nodded, she asked,

"What happens to a soul if you don't retrieve it? What becomes of it?"

"Their energy is gathered into what is around them. They fade away and are gone." He could sense there was more she wanted to know so he waited to take another bite of the sandwich.

"Does the soul know? That it is ending?"

Well, we're in this deep, he thought, why not go a little deeper? "Unfortunately, the soul is all too aware that its existence is coming to an end." He stopped to see how she would handle that. When she nodded, he continued. He tilted his head toward Joshua at the table, and said softly, "He feels when each soul exits the body it inhabits, when their living entity dies. If it's a painful death, he feels the pain. A peaceful one is easier. He also feels the souls diminish. Those are the worst for him."

The color drained from her face as she thought what that must be like to experience. She looked at Joshua, realizing then what had happened earlier, and she shook her head. "All this, it has to be taking its toll on him."

Azrael nodded.

"That explains why he's so driven to find answers."

Again, Azrael nodded. "It's harder on him when he remains here, on the planet. Takes more out of him than when he remains..." Azrael pointed vaguely up.

"Then why does he stay down here? He should be..." she looked up as though through the ceiling, "up... there... managing this at a safe distance."

"So, we've been telling him."

"Oh."

"Each soul is precious, and we've already lost too many," Azrael said. "He wants to remain close to the situation. He feels responsible for each and every one of them. It's his show, after all, as they say in your Hollywood."

They finished their sandwiches in silence. She took the plates to the kitchen and returned to sitting beside him.

He smiled. "You have that look again."

"How many lives have I lived?"

"Seventeen in the last two thousand years." It was Christian who answered. "You did one stint on another planet. Took about one hundred Earth years in heaven afterwards before you opted back in."

"Wow. Seventeen lives."

"In between, when you're in heaven, you can remember them all and reconnect with souls you've interacted with," Azrael said. And then watched all the color drain from her face, and she fainted. Again.

Oops, he thought, probably shouldn't have said that. Too much information.

*****

Earth year 1916

A year ago, Jenna Taylor joined the queue of other young women departing for France. She had received a letter from her younger brother in a hospital unit across the Channel. A doctor included a note, saying only that he would not recover from his wounds and could not endure the crossing back to England. Against the protest of her parents, she volunteered and joined the French field hospital staff. She was 20 years old, no longer innocent to the horrors of the Great War. Her family had just buried her older brother.

She did not reach her younger brother in time. She could not comfort him in his last hours. Nor could she accompany his body home. She remained in France, moving with the medical staff wherever she was needed. Farm-raised, strong-hearted, resolved to do whatever she could for the boys from home, she endured the hardships and losses, quietly conflicted over the ones who were able to be sent home.

The week-long shelling became more intense all through the night and morning. On the first day of July, the orders to advance were given. The casualty clearing station was a sea of screams and blood and morphine induced moans. Jenna, along with two other nurses, were assisting a surgeon performing an amputation. Their morphine supply ran out an hour ago. The young lad's screams were nearly unbearable.

"You must hold him still!" the surgeon

shouted. Blood squirted in an arc across his face. "I can't tie off this artery if you can't hold him!"

Jenna looked up as another man, oddly wearing civilian clothes, placed his hands on each side of the boy's head. "I can help," he said calmly. The boy screams quieted, and he went limp in their hands. Jenna's eyes flicked from the boy's still form to the eyes of the man holding his head. "He must have lost consciousness," he said, and he withdrew to watch the surgeon finish. He remained near, his face pale and worn.

Jenna washed her hands and dried them, watching the man as he scanned the makeshift surgery tent. She approached, reaching her hand to his arm, and said, "Are you looking for someone?" He looked out of place not being in uniform. He sounded English, but not quite. His brown hair was certainly cut in the latest style from back home, his suit screamed Savile Row. A gentleman searching for someone, brother most like judging by his age.

When he turned to her, his eyes were still wide, struck, she thought, by the horror in front of them. She was surprised how numb she had become to it all.

"How much longer can this go on?" He shook his head, realizing he spoke aloud when he hadn't meant to do so. "I'm sorry, what did you say?"

"Are you looking for someone?" she repeated her question. His eyes were now focused on her.

"Nurse Taylor, I need you!" The surgeon was impatient. The bombing had ceased, for now. The medical staff had worked through the night, no sleep, no meals. Only a brief cup of tepid tea kept most of them on their feet. "I'm sorry," she said, and turned away.

Jenna turned her attention to her duties but noticed the strange man remained in the triage station. His manner was quiet, his eyes taking in everything. He reminded her of someone affected by shell-shock, here but not here. Someone will get him sorted, she thought, and turned her attention away. It would be more than two years before she encountered the man again.

Earth year 1918, November the 11th

The Cease Fire was finally achieved. The medical staff paused briefly to cheer; spirits flowed freely. It would still be some time before all the injured were sent home and the medical staff could return as well. Jenna Taylor was in no hurry to return to England. She stepped outside to listen to the silence. She raised her eyes to the sky and sent a brief prayer up to heaven. "Thank you," she whispered to a dreary grey sky.

When she lowered her eyes back to the scene around her, she found a man observing her. They both experienced that flair of recognition which comes at first without comprehension.

"The Somme," she said finally, when her memory filled in the details.

"The field hospital," he said, nearly at the

same time. He smiled and nodded, acknowledging her.

"It's finally over," he said. He stepped nearer.

"Did you ever find who you were searching for that day?" she asked. Unfathomable. How is this man here, once again? Looking so very much the same as when she first saw him.

He held her eyes for a long moment. Reached up to touch her cheek, softly stroking the curve of her jawline. "Yes, I think I have."

*****

Monday, July 6 - evening

Julia awoke in the bedroom. Again. "Why do I smell pizza?" And what was with these dreams? They felt so real.

"Christian figured out how to order pizza. Pepperoni, olives, extra-large, stuffed-crust," Joshua said. "It just arrived. So did the rest of the crew. Coming?" He made her laugh by making his eyes shift from brown to green to blue and back to the brown she preferred. With a smile, he coaxed her back to the kitchen. "You're doing fine," he whispered to her as they walked down the hallway. "Better than most who learn the truth."

Close to midnight, Chamuel waited until the girl went into the bedroom to rest. He had been studying the girl, and her interaction with everyone else. Her energy levels rose and fell depending on who was closest to her. They spiked astronomically whenever she was near Joshua, and her levels were off the charts at the slightest touch between them.

Chamuel and Joshua were for the moment alone in the living room. Keeping his voice low, he said, "I need to speak with you."

Joshua looked up from the screen he was using, raised his eyebrows in question. It was unusual for Chamuel to be so forward, more of a behind the scenes guy. "What about?"

"The girl." He looked away, uncomfortable putting himself forward and uncomfortable with what he knew he must say. Finally raising his eyes to Joshua, he said, "You can't have her. Her soul, I mean. You can't merge with her." He had Joshua's full attention and watched a flash of fire flicker in his eyes.

"She has a name," Joshua said. His eyes shifted down the hall toward the bedroom. The energy in the room dropped significantly when she left, leaving behind a cold vacant feel. He was puzzling out that feeling when Gabriel suddenly materialized in the apartment.

"We will discuss this later, Chamuel," Joshua said. "Gabriel, what do you need?"

*****

Christian and Joshua were the only ones who stayed in the apartment that night, left with the task of monitoring the effects of everyone's field efforts. Ariel, with assistants, was shoring up damaged ecosystems, trying to bring more of Earth into balance. Raphael was out wandering the streets of Minneapolis, redirecting lost travelers and the lost souls who were on Azrael's suicide watch. Raphael's assistants were scattered far and wide, in all the major cities around the globe. Gabriel had arrived to ask for Chamuel's assistance sorting above. Joshua was relieved not to have to continue the discussion Cham had begun.

Christian made himself another cup of coffee. "Want one?" At Joshua's nod, he set the Keurig up to go again. "I like this thing."

He set the coffee in front of Joshua.

"Out with it," Joshua said. "You've got something you want to say, I can tell."

"Azrael says the girl remembers more every day she's around us," Christian said. "That's why she faints. The shock of it. She's putting together her other lives."

"She has a name. Why won't any of you use it?" His eyes flashed.

"That's only her current name, Josh." Christian paused. "And you know she can't return to this lifetime when this is over. We *will* have to pull her out. Reassign her." He could tell Joshua was getting too invested in this girl. He'd seen it twice before and that was enough to know the signs. *Train's about to derail into a hell of a wreck.*

"But she's doing so well, accepting everything," Joshua said. "It is possible we could just walk away. She's smart enough to know not to tell anyone. About all this."

But Joshua was trying to convince himself as

much as Christian. I should not have brought her back to this lifetime. Should have waited for another one to prevent. Instead, I resurrected her, and now we're messing with Julia's life, and her head. And I'm the only one feeling guilty about it. He thought the others had been too distracted to notice his feelings. Guess not. We've been a tight knit group for far too long. And I'm not being fair to either Christian or Azrael. They both feel a responsibility toward Julia. At least they wanted to do what they felt was right by her soul. If she needed to be pulled out... His line of thought stopped when Christian interrupted.

"I've been talking to Chamuel." He looked pointedly at Joshua, and judging by the clenching of his jaw, knew Chamuel had broached the subject with Joshua as well. "I did some digging into her file. Seventeen lifetimes in the last two thousand years alone makes hers a fairly old soul, Josh. I did some further digging into the archives. She predates you. She could be as old as your father. I know what you're thinking, and I have to recommend you not try it."

"Why? That's what I don't understand. Cham said the same thing." Joshua's voice was low. He really didn't want to discuss this. He had not had time to think things through himself. This flood of suicides was wearing him down, depleting him. It was difficult to focus on anything else. He felt the need to merge with another soul, soon. And he knew Christian knew it. If they all agreed to pull

Julia out, why not merge with her? Her soul seemed to like me, he thought with a slight smile, remembering its playful probing by the river.

"Cham says she's really powerful. Maybe even as strong as you." Christian's voice trailed down to a whisper. He wanted to shout, 'She touched you while you were glowing pretty fucking hot,' but he held back.

"I think *that* is a point in favor of the idea," Joshua said. "We're all leaning toward the idea of drastic measures here. Based on insights gained from Julia, I'll remind you. You, more than anyone else, knows what this will do to me. I need to merge. If we have to pull her out, why not merge with her?" Joshua stood up and walked into the kitchen to rinse his coffee cup.

Christian followed him. Standing at the sink, avoiding eye contact with Joshua, he said, "We're all afraid that if you did this... We're concerned which of you would come out dominant."

"But –" Joshua stopped, gathered his thoughts. "She can't be as strong as that. Seriously?"

"Josh, she's been around longer than you. She should have faded over time, but she hasn't. Quite the opposite. I think you need to examine your feelings. For her. I think you're emotionally attached and it's clouding your judgement." Christian looked him in the eye and waited a moment before continuing. "You haven't been with anyone for a very long time, old man. Every soul needs some element of love. Even yours. It's only natural for you to feel...

desire for her. She's quite pretty. I say get it over with, deal with it. You're entitled to a booty call now and then."

Christian turned to the sink to rinse his coffee cup. He missed the fire flashing in Joshua's eyes, but he sure as hell felt Joshua's fist slam into his jaw. The coffee cup shattered on the kitchen tile as Christian hit the floor. "Hell, old man. That was not called for!" He glared at Joshua from the floor.

"Julia is not a... How could you even think such a thing?" Joshua offered Christian his hand and pulled him up off the floor.

Christian decided to hold his tongue. He had hoped to get Joshua to open up, talk to him. He knew Joshua was conflicted over the whole situation and he really only wanted to help. He began picking up shards of the cup.

Joshua returned to the table. He sat with his elbows on the table, head in his hands. He reeled in his anger, and his internal fire. When he finally spoke, his voice was calm. "I admit I was not thinking about possible consequences when I resurrected her. Michael's always telling me I'm too impetuous. Well, this time he was right. I didn't think. Messing up her life - that's all on me."

Christian sat down across from him and still remained quiet.

"You're right, too, Chris." Joshua looked him in the eye. "I do have feelings for her. I feel guilty for messing up her life. It's not a fair hand she's been dealt. And yes, I do admire her. She's handled this better than any other we've had to brief. You have to admit that." When Christian nodded, he continued. "She's kind, sweet, funny, smart –"

"Don't forget pretty," Christian threw in.

"As you would point out – in this timeline, yes, she is." He heaved a big sigh. "If she is as strong as Chamuel thinks she is, well, after all this time perhaps she's earned it. Look at what she's been through in this timeline alone. My gut feeling still tells me she is a good soul. She deserves a fair shake."

"Josh, I'm sorry I said… what I said before."

Joshua waved off his apology. "You may not have been too far off base. I don't know," he said. "Look, I gotta clear my head. I'm going up. I need to speak to Az. Can you keep an eye on Julia?"

"Yeah, sure," Christian said. "What should I tell her if she wakes up?"

Joshua smiled. "Tell her I'll be back soon." He dematerialized.

"Heard that before, old man." Christian said to the empty room and returned to work.

*****

A knock on his Office door drew Joshua's attention away from the reports coming in from Earth.

"May I speak with you?" Chamuel hesitated just outside the open door.

Joshua waved him in. Might as well get this over with, he thought. I owe it to him to hear him out.

"I just would like to give you my impressions

of... Julia," he said, nodding at her name.

"I've already spoke with Christian about her." Joshua sighed, and flicked the screen in his hand to off. "I will need to merge with another soul before this gets too much. Christian seems to feel her strength is equal to one of the guardians."

"I have to agree with his assessment," Chamuel said.

"I –" Josh dropped his head and gasped. "Oh, hell."

Chamuel watched Joshua's aura ebb and flow, darker, then brighter, while he absorbed the pain of another soul lost, another one fading into the ether. "Joshua, when exactly was the last time you merged?"

Joshua looked directly at him, straightened up and took a deep breath. When he thought he could speak again, he said, "Nearly four hundred years ago."

Chamuel stared, eyes growing wider. It was worse than he thought.

"I'm all right, Cham. Just a bit tired," he said. "I'm going back down. I'll be sending Christian up to give everyone a full briefing. Everyone's gathering in the conference room."

Joshua waited until Chamuel left before he allowed his thoughts to return to that merge. He shuddered in revulsion, remember the sickening thoughts on that soul's mind. He shook his head to clear the thought and dematerialized.

*****

Joshua returned to the apartment only a few hours after he left it. He sent Christian up to assist with the full briefing. Gabriel had put out the call and brought all hands on-deck, so to speak. There were other guardians serving as 'archangels' on the other planets and moons scattered far and wide. These were recalled to assist with the crisis on Earth, and they needed to be brought up to speed. A solution needed to be found, one with the least collateral damage. He stared at the screens still running on the kitchen table, not really seeing them as his eyes blurred. He rubbed his eyes fretfully. *Holy Hannah, I am tired.* He hadn't felt this drained in a long time. A very, very long time. Not since... He had to think about it. Not since Chris was created. Could it really have been eight hundred years ago?

He walked back to the bedroom to check on Julia. She lay curled up on her side, her hair falling across her face. With the softest touch, he brushed the strands from her cheek. *Christian's right, she is pretty*. He gently traced the curve of her cheekbone and arch of her eyebrow. He withdrew his fingers when she shifted slightly in her sleep. He didn't want to wake her. She needs the sleep more than I do, he thought.

I need to rest, but what if she wakes up and walks out? Could call someone else down here, he thought, but that's such a bother. He sat in the chair, tried to get comfortable but was losing the battle to keep his eyes open. After a few minutes, he gave up and stretched out on the other side of the bed. He was sure he would feel the bed move if she stirred. He closed his eyes and felt himself sinking into sleep for the first time in...

Julia opened her eyes. The street light outside the bedroom window was enough light for her to see she was no longer alone in her bed. She tried not to move, watched him in the silence. He lay on his side facing her; his breathing was light and even.

"He sleeps," she whispered to no one but herself.

He murmured her name and reached for her hand, tucked it in against his chest with a quiet sigh. His face relaxed and lost the constant look of anxiety, for a little while at least. She watched him until her eyelids began to grow heavy again. Ever so softly, she brushed a strand of hair from his cheek, traced a line from his brow to his chin.

Julia drifted back to sleep.

*****

Earth year 1228 – the Holy Land

His father sent Joshua to return once more to Earth, to the lands where he was born.

"It just seems like the greater the number of humans in one area on that planet, the more territorial they get," Joshua said.

"They believe they are followers of your teachings," his father said. "Let me know if you need me to create a famine or pestilence. Just to knock some sense into them."

Joshua heaved a sigh. "Father, let me just try my way first."

"We've had to retrieve over a million souls from that region alone in the last seventy-five years. It's out of hand, Joshua. Azrael said over a thousand souls were lost, and..." he stopped, and shook his head. He looked Joshua in the eye. "I'm going to need to merge soon if this keeps up, and you know we don't need to lose even one more soul right now."

"I know, I know." His father was weakening. Chamuel felt it, too, and had warned Joshua. "I'm taking Michael with me. We'll figure something out."

Michael and Joshua arrived in Jerusalem. Joshua watched his previous teachings being distorted and used as justification of massacres of Jewish communities, civilians, and those of the Muslim faith. His words perverted to push economic and territorial agendas.

Acting as diplomatic envoys of Emperor Frederick II, their job was to attempt negotiating a treaty, to end the bloodshed. The Christian Crusaders wanted control of Jerusalem. They needed to convince the Muslim Saladin's nephew, Al-Malik al-Kamil to relinquish the city. Michael was the real diplomat between the two of them, but both he and Joshua used their influence as much as was possible without revealing their true nature.

Joshua accepted the use of a modest villa for the duration of his commission. They kept a small number of attendants within the villa, household staff necessary to keep rooms available for visiting dignitaries. And a few visiting guardians, Joshua thought, smiling wryly. He had requested the services of Gabriel and Uriel to act as envoys from al-Kamil, fingers in all the pieces of the pie, so to speak. Gabriel and Uriel had just left.

A young woman was clearing the table of the remnants of their lunch. Joshua watched her; his eyes drawn to the shape of her. Ja'elle. A very pretty name. He knew he mustn't speak to her. Her parents were very devout and strict. She could serve at table, and elsewhere in the house, but no man was allowed to address her directly. He respected her parents, but he had trouble convincing his eyes to stop following Ja'elle about the villa. There was something unique about her, drawing him in. He couldn't explain it. Not even to Michael.

He froze when she caught him in the act of staring. She held his eyes, drew a deep breath, and then dropped her eyes. As she took the remaining plates from the table, she turned slightly at the doorway to look back at him. A small smile played on her lips as she ducked her head again and fled the room.

Joshua let out a breath he was holding.

Michael frowned, and sighed loudly drawing Joshua's attention.

"What?" Joshua asked, trying to look nonchalant.

"You have that look in your eye," Michael said. "She's very pretty, but you know how her parents feel."

"I would never do anything to shame them or her," Joshua said. "I've never even spoken to her," he added hurriedly. He wracked his brains for anything to say to change the subject.

Michael rescued him. "We're never going to get this mess worked out, are we?" He stood and stretched. "I could use some exercise. Walk with me?"

Joshua nodded and followed him. They walked the streets, nodding to acquaintances. "How long have we been down here, Michael? A year already?"

"Nearly. At least we've brought about a truce. That ought to please your father," Michael said. "Chamuel said he has put off merging in hopes he won't need to," he added, eyeing Joshua discreetly, watching for his reaction. Chamuel had secretly told him Joshua's father was tired, diminishing. Joshua seemed unaware of his father's condition. Understandable, distracted by their mission down here. And Michael was starting to think there was more than a little distraction in the young woman working in the villa. A complication brewing. *We need to finish this and get out*, he thought. *Soon*.

The next morning Michael found Joshua at breakfast. "I'm needed..." He looked up, significantly.

"Sounds like it will take a few days, maybe even a week. Something brewing in the East," he said.

Joshua nodded to him. "I can handle it here for a while. Not much to do until Gabriel or Uriel returns anyway." He watched Michael leave with mixed feelings. *I never get much time alone anymore, but then I don't know what to do with myself when I am alone.*

He picked up his cup of fruit juice and went outside into the garden behind the villa. He took a seat on a bench and enjoyed the quiet of the garden, the scents of flowers and fruits, the buzzing of insects – it all lulled him into a sense of inner peace he rarely had the chance to experience. He sat back and let the morning sun caress his face, a gentle breeze played with his hair and made clay chimes sway, creating soft music in the background.

He opened his eyes to see Ja'elle approaching carrying a basket of pears. When he realized he was staring, he hastily dropped his eyes, meaning to keep them averted until she passed by. The breeze carried with it her scent. He couldn't deny how tantalizing it was. Pears, the meadow, her own rich scent all mingled. He looked up when he felt her pause just a few feet away. As if she willed it, their eyes locked. She shifted her basket to her other hand, and tentatively reached out to touch his cheek, gently tracing a line from his temple to his lips. She smiled when she heard his breath catch, and then continued into the villa.

The next morning, Joshua returned to the

garden. And waited. *I must speak to her*, he thought, unable to even consider the alternative.

Ja'elle emerged from the villa carrying her gathering basket. She paused when she saw Joshua seated in the garden. She felt a tremor run through her, not sure yet if it was caused by pleasure or fear, but it told her she was indeed alive, and something was awakening within her. She glanced at him, briefly catching his eye and inclining her head toward the orchard. She walked away quickly, keeping her eyes down as was seemly. A few minutes later, a quick glance behind her showed he was following but at a discreet distance. She tried and failed to keep a smile from her lips. She would have this man, whether her parents liked it or not.

By the time a treaty was finally reached, Joshua and Ja'elle were married. Not exactly with either of their parents' full blessing, but no one could deny they were two people very much in love. The evidence of their love was about to arrive. Joshua waited outside with Michael. His heart froze when Ja'elle's screams stopped. A wave of pain brought him to his knees.

"Joshua!" Michael ran to him. He helped him to his feet, and they both turned when Ja'elle's father appeared in the doorway. His face was stricken with grief, tears uncontrolled.

"You have a son. But Ja'elle... My wife says she will not recover," he sobbed.

Joshua broke away from Michael and ran into

the villa, to her side. He only had time to touch her cheek, kiss her lips one last time, and then, her soul separated from her body.

When Azrael arrived, Joshua was holding his son. Azrael was shocked to see the child alive, an unassigned soul.

"Joshua, you created a new soul." Azrael's voice was deeper and softer than usual, hushed almost, wondering.

"How is that even possible?" Joshua asked. He shook his head and said, "Azrael, please don't take her. He's going to need his mother."

"Your father needs a merge, Joshua. And soon. Chamuel says there isn't much time."

"I'll speak to him," Joshua said. "There must be some other way..."

"You will need to take her soul up with you. She will fade soon if she is not collected."

Joshua nodded, and turned to the soul of his heart waiting beside Azrael. "Ja'elle, come to me, love," he whispered and waited. The soul wrapped around him with light feathery touches resonating with love. Joshua's face contorted as he gave into tears. He dematerialized, arriving before his father with Ja'elle's soul.

"Why? Why this soul?" Joshua demanded.

"You cannot remain much longer on Earth, Joshua. This soul has tied you down there far too long." His father drew himself up as best he could manage. It took much of his remaining strength.

"Our child will need one of us," Joshua said. "If you won't let her return to raise my son, then I will remain on Earth for him."

"Joshua, you need to listen to me and not to your heart for once. I can't do this alone anymore. If you return to Earth, I must merge with her soul to remain in control of the Program." He waited for Joshua to think those words over. "Her soul then is lost to you forevermore."

"And if I stay?" Joshua whispered, dread filling his heart.

"I will allow you to return her to Earth, to raise your son."

"But only you can return her soul to her body," Joshua said, and then a chill ran over him as the full implications of his father words sank in. "You want to retire."

"Yes, son, I do. It is time for you to take up your legacy." His father paused. "I will allow you the ability to speak with this soul before you make your decision. You haven't much time."

Joshua swallowed a fist-sized lump in his throat. He nodded to his father, and then he beckoned the soul to walk with him in the garden outside The Office. Ja'elle's soul enveloped him once again and to his utter joy, he could hear her. He sat on a bench and listened, and gave her his promise. He rose with a heavy heart and returned to his father.

He met his father's eyes. "I will return shortly," he said, and dematerialized.

Azrael looked up when he appeared. He was gently rocking the baby, now swaddled in a blanket. "He's beautiful, you know."

Joshua nodded, blinking back tears. "You intend to wipe her memory before I return her?"

"It's for the best, Joshua. I am sorry," Azrael said. "Are you both ready?"

The breath Joshua drew in shook all of him. He was unable to speak. He remained very still while he beckoned Ja'elle's soul to leave him. He shivered from sudden cold and loneliness. Azrael communed with the soul briefly before Joshua reunited it with Ja'elle's body.

"What is your son's name, Joshua?" Azrael asked as he placed the boy in Joshua's arms.

Joshua looked down with tears in his eyes. He kissed his forehead, breathed in the scent of him. "Christian. His name is Christian.

He gasped when Ja'elle's hand touched his cheek, wiping away his tears. "Your son," he said as he relinquished him into her arms.

"Azrael, I have need of you above," he said, and he fled.

THE FIFTH DAY...

Tuesday July 7

The kitchen clock read 5:30 AM when Christian, Michael, and Chamuel returned to the apartment. Not seeing Joshua, Christian went to check the bedroom for Julia.

He came to an abrupt stop in the doorway. He shook his head, smiled to himself. Well, they look comfortable, he thought. Joshua and Julia were curled around each other, fingers entwined. That did not take as long as he thought it would. He went back to the kitchen where the others turned to him with questioning looks.

"He's sleeping," he said, trying to sound casual and keeping to a softer voice, afraid to awaken Joshua. If he needed sleep, it was worse than they all thought.

The others crept down the hallway to peer into the bedroom. Chamuel remained when

Michael returned to the kitchen.

"I can't remember the last time he slept," Michael said.

"World War One or Two?" Christian suggested, trying to think of the most taxing trials for the strength of God. "Or was it that mining explosion on Ravendune?"

Chamuel's observation was more than just watching two people sleep. He was watching the energy aura surrounding the bed. One energy field, not two. He bit his lip and nodded to himself. This changed things. Their breathing and heartrates were synched, their souls already prepared to merge. And he'd be willing to bet they were completely oblivious to it. He returned to the kitchen, going directly to Christian.

"Could you pull up Julia's complete file? I think we'd better learn as much about her as possible," he said. He met Christian's eyes, and nodded, wanting him to get right on it. He watched Christian's fingers start flying on his keyboard.

"Are you saying..." Michael was too shocked to complete his question.

Chamuel nodded, solemn eyes turning to each of the others. "It will happen. They will merge. They're already synched. This... I do not understand the manner of this."

"You think they've interacted before this?" *Holy hell, that would mean...* Michael was quick to grab a screen. "Send it to this one, too, please." His mind was racing. Joshua only ever made rare appearances on Earth. Souls changed physical forms with each lifetime, different skin or hair color, sometimes different sexes. He could not recall a time when Joshua could have encountered another soul long enough to... Then he looked at Christian. And found him looking right at him, waiting.

"My mother," Christian whispered.

Michael nodded.

"Why didn't they merge when that timeline ended?" Christian asked.

Michael just shook his head. It wasn't that he didn't know the answer. He did. It was just not his place to tell Christian, or anyone else for that matter. It was Joshua's secret, to tell or keep. And hers. Looking back at the screen, studying her soul's timeline, comparing it to his memory.

Aw, holy hell. This really changed things. He knew the details that had been redacted from her file.

*****

Sunlight streaming through the window warmed his skin and woke Joshua. Julia was sleeping on her side beside him, in his arms. He didn't want to leave the brief nest of peace he had found, but he sensed the return of others in the front of the apartment. As quietly as possible he slid off the bed, trying not to wake her. A quick glance at the clock beside the bed told him it was still very early. A soft snap of his fingers and he was in a clean shirt and jeans. He looked at his bare feet. Another snap brought socks and shoes. *Concentrate, Josh, old man. You have a universe to run.*

He stopped just before reaching the kitchen. *Looks like headquarters has been brought to Minneapolis*, he thought. All heads snapped up to him when his presence was noted. Michael, Christian, Ariel, Raphael and Chamuel opened their mouths to speak.

"Coffee, first," he said, silencing them all. He wanted a few minutes to prepare himself for this day. A little time alone in his head.

"Need help?" Christian asked, smiling.

"No, I think I have this machine figured out, thanks," he said. I hope. I'll look like a fool if I ask for help now. Water, little pod, mug, button. Whoohoo, it worked, he thought as coffee started drizzling into his mug. The old man can learn new tricks. Triumph over a coffee machine. He reached for creamer in the fridge while the machine did its thing. He hid in the kitchen, drinking half the mug. Ready. Decision day. They needed to put something in motion today. Too many souls lost yesterday and through the night. *All right then*. He squared his shoulders and joined the others at the table.

"Lay it on me," he said. "Christian, you first." Get the facts over with while the coffee kicks in, he thought. Besides, he liked Christian's voice the best in the morning.

"The average global suicide rate used to be thirteen out of one hundred thousand." Christian shifted in his chair before continuing. "In much of Europe, the rate is currently thirty-four per one hundred thousand, Japan is at thirty-eight, the United States at forty-five." He looked at the others. "The rates are increasing daily." He shot a quick look at Joshua. "I'm sorry, old man."

Joshua smiled at the title Christian slipped in. He was the only who got away with it.

"Is the homicide rate up?" Michael asked.

Christian consulted his data. "Not nearly as much, no. In spite of the rising socio-political tension increasing exponentially in the last..." he paused with a look at Joshua, "in the last four years, there has only been a slight increase in hate crimes. People are just offing *themselves*."

Joshua nodded. Christian's hesitation was another nod to Julia's input regarding the political situation in the United States. "All right. Chamuel? What have you got?"

"Depression is widespread, across all continents, urban and rural communities. Unemployment is up world-wide. The economy was booming in the States, so the unemployment figures didn't fit. I did some checking. Snooping actually. And I found employers weren't firing or letting people go. People are just walking away from jobs." He paused, rubbed his face. He was tired, too. Chamuel was definitely not used to being on active ground duty. "The auras of the largest metropolitan areas have become so dark it's been hard to penetrate to see the individual humans. I've been down on the streets." He shook his head, staring at the memories of bleak souls wandering darker paths. "I don't know when I've seen it so dark. It's as if the humans are shunning each other, closing themselves off from interaction. Crawling under shells and behind defensive walls. Caveman mentality..." He left off when Azrael materialized in the living room.

Joshua gave him a reproving look for entering in that manner.

"What? I figured she'd still be sleeping at this hour," he said, joining them at the table.

"Anything to report?" Joshua said, rolling his eyes at him.

"Not good. Most of the souls I interviewed during the night do not want to return to Earth." He heaved a sigh and continued. "Too crowded was the most common reason. No peace, discrimination for so many reasons and fear of catastrophic weapons being used by the various political entities." He looked around the table with bleak eyes. Joshua had never seen Azrael so disturbed. "I've never seen so many souls slink off into hiding once they reach heaven. We will have a hard time convincing some of them to ever take another turn at planet life."

"We all know heaven can support them all, but they used to be happy on Earth," Raphael said.

"Ariel?" Joshua sought everyone's input.

"I'm sorry, I should have been paying better attention to Earth. My fascination with Ravendune has interfered with my duties here. The planet is, well, basically a mess. The polar icecaps are decreasing, air pollution – let's just say I'm glad I don't need to live here regularly. Did you know they are putting their garbage on barges and setting them adrift in the ocean?" Ariel shuddered. "I took care of a few of those and have others searching for more." Ariel glanced around the table, had everyone's attention. "I'm afraid there are just too many humans on the planet. Julia is right."

"So, population decrease is your recommended course?" Joshua asked. He watched Ariel nod.

"I see no other way." Christian said. "Anyone else?"

All nodded in agreement.

"What kind of numbers are we talking," Joshua asked, looking to Christian but wasn't surprised when Ariel answered instead.

"Earth is currently at seven-point-nine billion souls. We're suggesting returning it to four billion, and then controlling population growth to maintain it under four and a half billion." Ariel said, receiving a nod from Christian.

Josh closed his eyes.

Holy hell.

This is going to hurt.

Julia stood in the hallway, just out of sight of everyone gathered in her kitchen. Overhearing the discussion, she tried to process it. Earth is going to need a reduction in population. And immediately or the population will keep taking care of it themselves, to great loss, she thought to herself. Thinking of the lost souls from the increased suicides, gone forever. But they are now contemplating even greater numbers of people being killed.

Killed with no choice in the matter.

Julia felt the shaking start in her jaw and it quickly took over her entire body. Her mind raced, freaking out. This can't be happening. This can't be real. They were starting to sound like terrorists plotting to kill half the world's population.

She lunged for the door, escape the only thing in her mind. I've got to warn someone, anyone.

Joshua caught the door before she could get it fully open and slammed it shut, pressing her back against it. She screamed and pummeled him with her hands. He caught her hands and pinned them above her head. "Stop, Julia, please stop this." He emitted a glow as he stared deep into her eyes. "This has to be. You know this is the only way."

She gasped when she saw him glowing. Powerful light flooded the room, coming from his body. In another lifetime, she had once seen him fully manifested like this. *The dreams*. "I've seen you before. You saved me, in the stable yard, from another man..." her voice trailed off, her eyes lost focus, her breath came in gasps.

"Joella," he whispered a name returning to his memory. He released her hands and pulled her to him as she fainted. "Joella," he murmured to himself as he quelled the light emanating from him. He turned to see the others staring, mouths gaping. Realization staggered him. "Azrael? You tampered with my memory?"

Azrael slowly nodded. He stepped closer to Joshua, laid a hand on his shoulder and said, "You asked me to do so."

"Why? Why would I do that?" Joshua took a deep breath and let it out slowly, trying to think, trying to remember.

"Shall I restore your memory?" Azrael asked, looking down at Julia. "Your memories of your interactions with this soul?"

Joshua closed his eyes, sinking down within himself. His physical body felt the warmth of hers in his arms. He realized then *what* he had experienced lying next to her during the night. His soul had recognized hers, even if his mind had not. "Yes," he said without opening his eyes.

Azrael's hand sent a vibration through Joshua's body, awakening long suppressed memories. The vibration passed through Joshua and on to Julia, allowing her memories to fall into place as well, fully awakening her soul. When Joshua opened his eyes again, Azrael said, "Let me take her to the bedroom. She will need some time to sort it all out. It's best she sleeps a while longer."

Joshua nodded and watched as Azrael carried Julia to the bedroom. It's going to take *me* a while to sort it all out. Lacking the motivation to do anything else, he slid down the door to sit on the floor and dropped his head into his hands. He was, literally and figuratively, floored.

Michael watched him for several minutes and

finally sat down next to him. Joshua was more to him than the God role he had assumed at his father's resignation. They'd been through so much together over the last two thousand years, they were more like brothers.

"Why didn't you tell me?" Joshua asked.

"I didn't know this was her," Michael replied. "In the beginning, anyway."

"When did you figure it out?"

"Only a little while ago. When you were sleeping." Michael hesitated. "Chamuel could tell that you were already synched with her soul." He watched Joshua nod. "What can I do?"

Joshua finally looked Michael full in the eyes. "I don't know." His voice was full of dread, his eyes full of pain and regrets. His soul burned with memories of heartache, longing and loneliness. He turned from Michael to stare down the hallway, toward where Julia lay sleeping. "Until this is over, we answer every question she asks. We owe her that."

*****

The kitchen acquired another table. And more electronics. When Julia finally emerged from the bedroom, she went straight for coffee, waving everyone to silence, to leave her alone with her thoughts. She noted the pained look on Joshua's face as she turned away from him. Coffee finally in hand, she sat next to him and felt him sag into her. She leaned against him, drawn to him, but unable to put any of her thoughts into words. It will have to wait a bit, she thought. My kitchen looks like an overly crowded television news station. She listened while Christian brought her up to speed and heaved a tremendous sigh of resignation when he finished. They really meant to do this. Population reduction. But she knew more now. Her memories of timelines on Earth and all the changes that have occurred in two thousand years, her time in heaven, even that horrible timeline on that other planet. *That* memory, I could have lived without, she thought. A shudder ran through her, and she was relieved to feel Joshua lean closer.

"Before we begin, we need to establish another habitable planet." Christian said. "I've located two very similar to earth. Ariel is checking them both out and will send a report soon."

"I suggest we use both if possible. No sense tempting fate," Michael said.

"I agree," Joshua said.

"Are there any that could end up with high human densities like the major industrial cities here on Earth?" Julia asked. "Smaller ones, moons maybe?"

"What are you getting at?" Joshua looked interested.

"I'm assuming Christian's virus will affect Earth's population randomly. Correct?" She looked to Christian, who nodded. "Unfathomable as it may seem, some people do like to live in large cities. With tons of activity all close at hand. Is it possible to poll the souls as they return to heaven to see what their preferences are and place them accordingly? Let them create the world they need." Julia blinked, shaking her head. "I can't believe I'm having this conversation. Again."

Azrael was nodding his head. "Yes, that would help. Shift souls to the appropriate planets, rather than random as we have been doing. Could work." He gave Julia a nod of approval. I should have thought of that, he thought. A point in her favor, all those lifetimes spent here. "Once Earth has recovered more open spaces, many will want to return." Azrael was nodding, already visualizing. "How do we ensure the population doesn't grow out of proportion again?"

"I guess we'll have to adjust the reproductive process, limit the number of pregnancies," Joshua suggested. His mind flashed back to the motel he'd seen next to the shopping district. The flashing neon sign changed to – Motel Earth ~~Vacancy/No Vacancy. He looked around to see the others nodding in agreement.

"Will the souls forgive this? What you are planning to do? Rip them out of lives. Away from loved ones." Julia was thinking out loud and looked up to see all eyes turned to her. The silence was profound. *I've hit a nerve,* she thought. She turned to Joshua for an answer, but it was Michael who spoke.

"Memory wipes are done when a soul is reassigned. It makes acceptance come a bit more easily to the souls. And time spent in heaven with souls they were once attached to helps them recover their sense of peace." When she looked at him, he continued. "Most people," he waved a hand at her indicating her human form, "are not like you, Julia. Most don't fill in the gaps of their timelines. They remain ignorant of the real circumstances of all this until they are collected back to heaven." He caught a glance and nod from Joshua, so he continued. "It is human nature to create religion, a belief system, to explain things they do not understand. The human's construct of God has a history of righting the wrongs on this planet. The people believe terrible things happen because their god, or gods, will it. We need the ones who remain on Earth to believe once again. Believe it is his will that brings about the reduction in their numbers."

"In order for them to accept it, you mean," Julia said. "So, the disaster has to be a real event. You can't just," she waved her hand upward, "make a few billion people dematerialize up to heaven." When Michael nodded, she asked, "How do we deal with all the... bodies... of the departed?"

Again, all eyes froze on her. It had seemed a practical question. A detail. A huge detail they should have considered.

"What would you suggest?" Christian wanted her opinion, wanted to know what would be expected by current cultural standards.

"Well, cremation would be the most practical," Julia offered.

"And the most logical if we are using a virus," Ariel added. Heads started to nod.

Joshua turned to Christian with raised eyebrows. "What can you work up?"

Christian blinked a few times, thoughts racing for ideas, when plans entered his mind coming from Ariel. "Ariel, do you think that would work?"

Ariel nodded, already contemplating the number of guardians needed to move both the bodies and the souls, reuniting them on new planets, altering memories. Only guardians have the ability to retain their forms while dematerializing. The bodies and souls would still have to be collected here on Earth, and then resurrected elsewhere. Right now, the elsewhere is what Ariel needed to establish, and quickly. "I'll get my team on it." Ariel forgot about protocol and simply dematerialized in front of Julia.

Julia turned to Joshua. "And what will this do to you?" The look on his face made her wished she had not asked.

"It's going to fucking hurt." It came out as a whisper.

Everyone remained locked in their own minds, silent acknowledgement of his burden.

A chime from Michael's wrist unit drew everyone's attention.

"Ariel's pretty excited," Michael said with a smile. "Christian, stay here. Joshua, we're needed to go inspect a planet and a moon. You, too, Az. If this is going to work, Christian, we need very careful choreography."

Josh leaned in close to Julia, spoke softly in

her ear. "I'll be back as soon as I can."

After their departure, the apartment felt hollow with just Christian working at the kitchen table. Julia fidgeted, washed up coffee mugs and tidied the apartment. When she ran out of things to keep her distracted, she sat down at the table across from Christian. She watched him, the shape of him, the tilt of his head as he worked, how his fingers moved across the keyboards. He looked up when he sensed her studying him. Her merged memories whirling chaotic in her head settled into place at his shy smile. She reached across the table, cupped his cheek in her hand. "Do you remember me?"

Christian closed his eyes, leaned into her hand and sighed. At her touch his soul recognized hers. He opened his eyes, could only nod. He swallowed a hard lump in his throat. "You look different, but I *know* you. I look into your eyes and I see my mother." He blinked unexpected tears from his eyes and swallowed hard again.

She smiled through moist eyes. "I know you, too. I watched you grow up but now I feel like I've missed so much. So much of your life."

"Joshua would have made an excellent father," Christian said. "He *has* been an excellent father to me since I joined him," he corrected. He held her hand in both of his and brought it to his lips briefly. "There's never been anyone but you in his heart, you know. Why didn't he stay with us?"

"He's never told you?" She blinked and drew back, confusion evident by her expression. "But I thought you knew, that Azrael told you everything when he collected you."

Christian shook his head, waited for her to speak again.

"I died giving birth to you, Christian. When Joshua brought me before his father, I was given a choice. I could either merge with the Caretaker, to remain in heaven as a part of him forever, or to return to you and a lifetime without Joshua. He needed Joshua. I wasn't important to him, only a source of energy. As much as Joshua wanted to, he couldn't remain on Earth to raise you. He persuaded his father to let me return if that was my choice, and he agreed to accept the role his father held."

"You gave up being one with the Caretaker, to be with me?" Christian took a deep breath and blew it out forcefully, trying to work that thought through his mind.

She nodded. "My memory was wiped. All I knew was that I had a beautiful baby boy, and it was enough. You were enough, Christian."

Christian's brow creased. "I don't understand how Joshua could stand to be parted from you–"

She interrupted him. "Joshua promised me that once he assumed his father's role, I would be his final merge. When his time as Caretaker comes to an end."

Christian had read her entire restored file. Seventeen lifetimes spent largely alone except the few times his parents' souls mysteriously managed to find each other. Briefly. Two thousand years of hit and miss. The last eight hundred years by their choice. For him. For him to experience one complete lifetime. Something Joshua and Julia never had the chance to experienced together. Separated until Joshua was ready to step down and hand the reins of the universe to him, his only son. His eyes once again filled with tears when he looked Julia in the eye. "It's so unfair. And now," he stopped to wave his hand at all the equipment, "all this. And when it's done..." He shook his head. "No, it's not right."

She took his face in both of her hands, wiped fallen tears away with her thumbs. "It's the end that counts, Christian. In the end, it will be all right." She placed a soft kiss on his forehead. "Christian, I need to go visit Gran, before it's too late. I won't be long. Don't let Joshua panic." She said the last with a smile, knowing he would anyway.

Christian stared after her for a long time. *There's got to be a way.*

*****

Julia sat in a chair next to her grandmother's bed, holding her withered hand in hers. She dozed off, lulled to sleep by the quiet hum of the fluorescent light fixtures in the room. And the lack of organized chaos that was happening in her apartment. When she opened her eyes, both Joshua and Azrael were in the room with her.

"Sorry. I fell asleep," she said.

Joshua shook his head, stalling her from further apology. "I just grew worried when you didn't return."

Julia looked at Azrael. "She won't survive the virus, will she?"

He shook his head. It was enough of an answer.

"Would you like to speak with her again. Before Az takes her up?" Joshua asked. He didn't want her worrying about her grandmother's fate once the virus was released tomorrow. He would spare her that agony.

She looked at Joshua. "You can do that? She hasn't spoken in over six months."

As he approached the bed, he began to emanate light. He closed his eyes and lay a hand on Gran's forehead. After a moment, they both opened their eyes. Julia watched a smile flood her grandmother's face. "You're beautiful," Gran said.

Joshua smiled down at her. "Julia is here."

"Oh, I have been so worried about her." Gran turned her head then and found Julia holding her hand. "Child, you gave me quite a fright the last time you were here." Gran looked back to Joshua and asked, "Will she be all right, now?"

"Yes. I will make sure of it," he said.

"Good. She's very special, you know?" Gran looked at Azrael. "I'll be ready in a minute. I want to speak to Julia alone, please." She waited until Azrael and Joshua left. "Julia, you don't have to worry about me any longer. I'm going to be with your grandfather now."

"Oh, Gran..." Emotions choked off her words.

"It's okay, now, dear."

"Will you tell Dad I miss him? And Mom, that I love her?" Julia blinked back tears.

"They know, dear. They know." Gran squeezed her hand. "Now, go send that man back in here to show me where I'm to go. I never imagined Death was so handsome."

Julia kissed her for the last time on the cheek and slipped out to the hallway. "She's asking for you, Azrael."

Azrael nodded to her, and then waited for Joshua to nod before entering Gran's room.

"She's the last family I had." Julia said, blinking back tears. She looked at Joshua. "Will she know me if I see her in heaven?" Julia smiled through tears when Joshua nodded. "Will you know my name when we meet again?" she asked.

"Wherever we are, when we meet again, I will know you."

THE SIXTH DAY...

Wednesday July 8

Christian released the virus in the early morning hours. He targeted the major airports to allow for the maximum spread of the virus in the shortest amount of time. The virus would only be active for thirty-six hours before it mutated to produce only flu-like symptoms. He charted the release on flights which would allow for a random spread so that all continents and political entities would bear the burden in equal proportions. He's *that* good with numbers.

On a whim, Christian had developed an additional quirky virus which he could have used to target specific individuals, but Joshua vetoed the idea. Joshua was convinced they needed to let the politics sort themselves out. Some parts of the human condition were just that – human. They could reduce the numbers, hope the conflicts lessened, but rewriting the entire human code wasn't something Joshua wanted to tangle with. He'd watched his father go down that particular rabbit hole of madness.

"We just have to hope that a massive worldwide calamitous event will open their eyes," Joshua said. "Maybe make them value life and each other more than they do now."

"But –" Christian was saying.

"No." Joshua silenced him. "There will be enough panic happening. Targeting all of the political leaders will convince the sci-fi fanatics that they are under an alien attack. Focus, Christian. Repeat after me. Natural Phenomenon."

"Fine. But I'm not deleting the program," Christian said. "You never know. Might come in handy. Some day."

Off-world, everything was set in motion. Two alternate planets much like Earth and one moon were ready to receive souls departing Earth. The guardians were busy creating necessary infrastructures and adjusting ecosystems. The moon chosen was to act as an intergalactic hub for travelers and was being written into the Programs running other planets. The moon was a tiny speck orbiting a planet covered in lethal gases in a system laying between many others, and the station would be crowded, noisy and teeming with many life forms.

Julia watched Joshua sink into the couch,

eyes glued to the television, watching the numbers rise. All of the sudden the words, "It's all in God's hands," took on new meaning. She watched shudders run through his body with increasing frequency.

The news channels were starting to cover the epidemic, running a continuous live-feed update on the bottom of the screen. Flashing new cities affected and updating numbers of the dead or hospitalized. A map of the world came up on the screen as they watched, mesmerized, unable to turn away from the television. The heavily affected cities showed up red. Arrows were drawn indicating the viral spread. Christian was meticulously tracking everything. Making sure his virus did not stray.

Joshua swallowed hard, never turning his eyes away. Remote in hand, he flipped from one channel to the next. Continuously. Flip. Flip. Flip. Until driven to distraction, Julia reached over the couch and took the remote away from him.

Men. She shook her head.

She lay a hand on his shoulder. "Can I get you anything?"

He reached up slowly and held her hand in place. "This is enough," he said softly. When she said nothing further, he finally tore his eyes away from the news to find tears welling in her own as she watched it. He held her hand to his lips. "I did this."

She turned hollow eyes to him. It made him cringe, adding to the guilt and weight of the situation.

"You said there was no other choice. That in the end..." her voice drifted away as the news anchor interrupted with the names of new cities with confirmed cases of the virus. Every hospital was desperately seeking volunteers.

"They are being taken care of, Julia," he said.

"I should be there, at the clinic," she said. "I am a nurse, Joshua."

He shook his head. "No. I can't protect you outside of this apartment." His grip tightened on her hand.

"It's who I am. You know this," she said softly. "I need to go in to the clinic."

Shaking his head, he silently mouthed the word, *no*. His eyes pleaded with her.

Joshua didn't need to read the numbers on the television, or on any of Christian's screens. He felt each victim of the virus as their bodies died, as the souls were released, all over the world. The deaths were taking their toll on him, his energy diminishing the more he endured. He endured their pain and suffering to lessen what each soul would suffer. It was the burden, the weight, he must bear in order to possess the power he wielded over the universe. Would he be strong enough to continue? Right now, he didn't know.

Watching Julia's face as she saw the rising numbers was almost harder on him. The tears fell silently down her cheeks without any attempt to wipe them away. So, he did. And drew her down to sit with him, touching his forehead to hers before pulling her into his arms as she wept.

She felt him shudder, shaking within. All these souls being ripped from lives they loved, and he feels every death and the collateral pain as if his own, she thought. “Oh, Joshua.” She had never felt so helpless, so useless.

*****

Urgent care at the Health Partners clinic, where Julia had worked, was swamped. It was never meant to function as a triage station for the number of people falling victim to this new virus sweeping the globe. Dr. Penny Nelson stood in the hallway, her hand over her masked mouth, staring dazedly at barely contained chaos.

“We can’t keep up,” she said to no one in particular.

“Doctor?” A passing nurse stopped before her.

“Kayla, have you called in everyone? What about Julia? I know she quit a few days ago, but we need more hands.”

“I’ll try her number again.” The nurse slipped behind a desk to grab her cell phone.

Dr. Nelson shook her head trying to shake off fatigue. She had come off the night shift when all hell broke loose late in the morning. She was working on three hours of sleep and it wasn’t likely she’d see her bed anytime soon.

*****

The afternoon wore on, and the apartment grew

quieter as duty began calling the guardians away. They drifted in and out, informing Joshua or Christian of pertinent details in heaven, Earth, or elsewhere. Most would stay for a few minutes to watch the screens or the television broadcast. The buzzing of electronics and the murmur of the news station continued.

Julia was alarmed by Joshua's silence. He'd returned pale from the bathroom. She suspected lunch no longer remained in his stomach. She caught Michael and Christian watching him as much as she did. She beckoned Michael to join her in the kitchen, leaving Joshua curled up on the couch.

"You've got to convince him to go up," she whispered to Michael.

"I've been trying, Julia!" Michael tried to keep his voice low. "I don't know what else I can say to make him leave the surface. He's stubborn beyond measure sometimes."

Julia nodded and went back to Joshua. "Joshua?"

He had shut his eyes and ears to the television and the screens. "Help me," he murmured as he reached for her hand.

"Joshua, you must go back up. At least for a little while," she said.

"I don't want to leave you here. What if–"

She shushed him with two fingers to his lips. "You're not going to do anyone any good if you don't get off Earth for a while." She coaxed him to his feet. "Go. For a few hours at least."

He stood close to her, his forehead against hers, avoiding eye contact. He did not want to admit how drained he was feeling. He sighed. "All right. I'll go. But not for long." His body trembled; his voice shook. He met her eyes for a moment, and with a kissed brushed to her cheek he stepped away. Joshua and Michael dematerialized, leaving Julia and Christian alone in the apartment for a change.

Christian let out a loud sigh of relief. "Thanks, Mom." He smiled when she looked at him, a smile playing on her face, too.

A few minutes later Christian slipped into the bathroom, and Julia heard her phone chime in her purse. (952)926-7477 was sending a text message. Kayla. The clinic. She shot a quick look down the hall to see if the bathroom door was still closed. She opened her messages and read: All Hands On Deck, Julia. Get Your Butt Down Here!!!

She scribbled a hasty note to Christian. A lie about groceries, she needed to buy some time if she was to be of any help at the clinic. She grabbed her ID badge and purse and ran out of the apartment. Her neighbor said she was always welcome to borrow her bicycle in an emergency. Today is an emergency if there ever was one.

Sorry, Josh, she thought as she raced to the clinic.

Twenty minutes later she was in scrubs, masked and setting IV lines.

*****

Joshua sagged against Michael when they arrived back in his Office. Michael half-carried him to the chair behind the desk and waited for Joshua to open his eyes again.

"You need to merge, Josh," Michael said softly.

Chamuel rushed into the room and breathed a huge sigh of relief upon seeing Joshua. "You need to merge! You almost didn't make it back."

"He's right. You're never going to make it through this." Michael voice shook, his face contorted with worry.

Joshua's eyes flashed. "Well, maybe I don't want to! Did either of you ever think of that?"

"What are you saying?" Michael asked, startled.

Joshua dropped his head into his hands, his elbows propped on the desk. Fighting what felt like ten thousand emotions and an overwhelming amount of weariness, he struggled to keep tears from his eyes. He failed to disguise the pain in his voice. "I'm just tired. Will you both give me a few minutes alone? Please."

Michael and Chamuel exchanged looks. At Chamuel's nod, Michael relented, and they left The Office, gently closing the door.

Joshua crossed his arms and lay his head upon them. Forgive me Father, I know not what to do, he thought, and closed his eyes.

Two hours later a frantic message came

through from Christian.

*****

Julia shut off the oxygen line and disconnected the IV. As she draped a sheet over her third patient lost in three hours, she lifted her eyes skyward as she so often did when seeking strength to carry on.

"Julia." Joshua stood in the doorway.

"Joshua..." she started.

He stopped her with a shake of his head. "I can't believe you came here. Of all places!"

She drew herself up and squared her shoulders, ready to argue her point. The look on his face was a mixture of anger, betrayal, hurt. "I'm sorry, Joshua. I'm a nurse. I had to come help."

He waved his hand to the covered body. "You can't help this. It will run its course, no matter what you or anyone here does."

"How can I make you understand that I *need* to help. They need me here."

Joshua was silent for a moment, then slowly stepped close and held her face in his hands, staring directly into her eyes. "I. Need. You. Come home with me. Please?"

She closed her eyes and sighed, too disheartened by the circumstances to resist him.

*****

Joshua and Julia barely made it through the apartment door before Christian grabbed Julia into a bear hug. And wouldn't let go.

"I'm sorry, Chris," she said, struggling to breathe. "Air, please."

Reluctantly he loosened his grip and let her go, wiping his eyes.

"Where is everyone?" Joshua asked. Michael had accompanied him down to Earth but was no longer present in the apartment.

Christian swirled a finger in the air and said, "Out and about. Azrael's swamped but maintaining. He's commandeered every available pair of hands for retrieval and resurrection." He heaved a sigh. "So far, so good."

Julia insisted on preparing something for them to eat. She wasn't up to anything complicated. Macaroni and cheese will have to do tonight, she thought. God... eating mac and cheese. Who would have thought?

When she finished dishes, she found Christian still in command of his monitors and Joshua stood leaning on the back of the couch with his eyes cemented to the television screen. She stood beside him and watched the numbers scrolling across the bottom of the news program.

"Holy Hell!" Christian exclaimed from the kitchen table. He tugged at his hair in frustration.

Joshua groaned and swayed on his feet. "Oh, ffff..." he moaned as pain ripped through him. His face contorted, he held his breath and his fingers clawed into the couch as he tried to remain on his feet.

Julia reached to support Joshua, shot a look at Christian seeking explanation.

"Village of Janem," he said. "Small community on North Supiori, Indonesia."

"The whole village?"

Christian nodded, his eyes bleak. "One hundred people." He looked at Joshua, "I'm sorry, Josh. No one was there. It's so out of the way, I never thought it would –"

"Chris, you can't predict everything," Joshua said, opening his eyes once again. He turned to brace his backside against the back of the couch, keeping Julia in the circle of his arms, he leaned his forehead on her collarbone. He sagged against her, drawing ragged breaths. After a few minutes his breathing returned to normal. He raised his head up and met her eyes again.

"You wear my cross." He indicated the necklace she wore.

"Yours?" Her eyes widened; her breath caught. What did he mean? She remembered the day she found the necklace. At the airport, she was flying somewhere and had just gone through the security screening. When she picked up her belongings out of the bin, she found the necklace in one of her shoes. She had looked around to see if anyone was looking for it, but even the security personnel seemed indifferent to finding its owner. *I've worn it ever since.*

He lifted her hair from the back of her neck, and slowly adjusted the lay of the chain. He held the cross on the tip of a finger and leaned in to place a kiss upon it. He lay it down against her throat and met her eyes. "Mine."

The cross burned with the heat of his fingers and his kiss. The cross.

Julia gasped as realization came to her. "Then, it's true," Julia said. "Oh, Josh. I don't know how you do it."

"Do what?" he asked, his eyes never leaving hers.

"Keep on carrying on. After... everything," she said, her voice dropping to a whisper. "What keeps you going?"

He slipped his arms around her, pulled her tight against him. "You do. You're my reality, my anchor, my fantasy. Every... God-damned... lonely... night." He sighed into her hair. "Azrael may have blocked my memories of you here on Earth, but your soul has haunted me for centuries."

She held him in silence. Words failed her. And words could not help him. She brushed silky strands of brown hair off his forehead and pressed her lips to it. "What can I do?"

He rested his forehead against hers. "May I kiss you? Please?" He felt her nod. He moaned softly, tilted her chin and claimed her lips. He pulled back and searched her eyes, looking for... he didn't know what. "I can't do this alone anymore." He crushed her lips with his, and when she moaned in response, he scooped her into his arms and walked down the hallway to the bedroom.

Christian froze in the act of typing a message to Michael, unsure what he should do. Collecting himself, he shook his head. *Nope. No way. I'm out of here.* He grabbed the tablets he needed and dematerialized leaving Joshua and Julia in the privacy they deserved.

Joshua kicked the bedroom door shut as he set Julia on her feet. Her lips parted beneath his, his tongue explored hers then tasted her jawline, the side of her neck. His hands slid under her t-shirt, pulling it up and over her head. Kissing her deeply he reveled in her light fingers unbuttoning his shirt, pulling it free from the top of his jeans and pushing it off his shoulders. He slipped the clasp to her bra and let it fall. He flung his shirt on the chair beside the bed.

Hands like wildfire stroked his skin sending him groaning, shudders of pleasure coursing through his body. Her kisses led a trail from his mouth to his throat, to his collarbone and down his breastbone. Her hands exploring, slid to the button of his jeans trying to free him from those as well.

With one hand around her waist and the other buried in her hair, he slammed their bodies together. The pulsing in his groin almost reaching an unbearable level of demand. He lifted her and lay her back on the bed, trying desperately to undo the button of her jeans. Fumbling at best.

She giggled at his frustrated attempt. "Josh, let me help –"

"Shhh, I can do this," he said while kissing

down her breastbone. "Oh, the hell with it," he muttered, and their clothing suddenly disappeared with a snap of his fingers. Skin to skin, he set about exploring every inch of her, setting her afire with his lips, his tongue, his demanding hands.

"Wait." She tried to stop him. "Christian's in the –"

He silenced her by claiming her mouth with his momentarily. "He's long gone, Jules." His hands slid up and down her sides, his lips following. "He couldn't handle imagining his parents in bed." His eyes lit with amusement, and then the hunger and loneliness of too many centuries without her.

Her eyes darkened; her voice grew husky. "Take me, Josh. Now. Please." Her hands urged him, her hips lured him, her eyes begged him for release from this aching need.

Her breath caught as he slid fully into her. She hooked her leg up and around his, pulled him tight when she sensed his hesitation. "Don't stop, Josh. Please, don't stop."

"I didn't know, Julia. You're sure?"

"Oh, love, it's a bit late now, don't you think?" she said, she sat up just enough to push against him, feel him deeper, playfully dragging him down to kiss him. "And it's not like we've never done this before."

"You are mine, now and forever," he murmured, losing himself completely in her embrace.

Darkness still reigned over the bedroom as Joshua

and Julia lay in each other's arms.

"Josh, you must go on. My lifetime –" she stopped and amended, "*this* lifetime, is done. I'm needed at the clinic. If I fall to the virus, I'm ready, Joshua." She forced him to meet her eyes. "We *will* meet again."

"I've spent so many centuries alone, wading through the dark, always looking for you. My father thought he was doing the right thing separating us the first time two thousand years ago. But he was wrong. So very wrong. I need you like I have never needed anything else, Julia."

She kissed him lightly, brief, soft. "I know, Josh. I know," she said. "I don't want to be separated from you. Ever again." She made him look at her. "Before this is over, you will need to merge. Take my soul, Joshua."

He pulled her tight to his chest, his cheek to her hair. Desperately needing to merge, wanting to make her a part of himself for eternity. They could continue as one until the time came when he would need to merge again. The promise he had made centuries ago, that she would be his last merge, came to mind. Yes, it would then be time to hand the Program over to Christian. His heart ached, and a soft cry escaped him. "Julia, I'm not ready. I want more of this. Holding you, making love to you." He sat up, holding her so he could look in her eyes. "I don't want to merge. Not with anyone. Not with you. Not yet. I want to love you. To live *with* you. I've been waiting all my life. For once in my life, I don't want to wonder if you'll still be here tomorrow or get whisked away from me again."

"How?" Julia asked. "You'll never make it through this. Not without merging. I can tell, Joshua." She clung to him, shaking with the shudders passing through him, weakening him.

They held each other in silence. Desperate strength, hearts pounding, every inch which could be pressed against the other tangled their two bodies into one. He held her face in his hands, kissed her deep, forever in its promise. When his lips released hers, she wiped tears from his eyes and cheeks. His voice shook.

"We face the virus together."

AND ON THE SEVENTH DAY…

Thursday July 9

Christian rematerialized in the apartment the next morning. It was early, so he was not surprised to find himself alone in the kitchen. He made a cup of coffee and quickly became engrossed in screens and tablets. He thought about checking in with Joshua, but his mind froze up at the thought of seeing Joshua and Julia (his parents!) in bed. Nope. I'll just wait for them to come out when they are good and ready.

The guardians had all maintained a steady pace through the night. Some checked in via their comm units, others materialized in The Office where Christian had fled, reporting to him. Christian checked the stats and noted that deaths due to the virus were decreasing. The virus was losing strength and the spread was halted by worldwide quarantines being enforced. The airports, bus and train terminals and all highways were literally closed to all travel. Christian frowned, studied the numbers and calculated they would still arrive at the goal. The virus even in its non-lethal stage will still remove some elderly and others of weakened immune systems. Christian wanted those souls free to choose another lifetime, hopefully one without pain or suffering.

*****

Josh and Julia walked to the clinic holding hands. A calmness had settled on them when they had reached their decision to volunteer at the clinic. Arriving around 6:00 AM, Julia checked in at the nurse's station. She introduced Joshua and asked that they be allowed to tend to the patients who would not recover. They both knew the virus would be active for twelve more hours. Neither thought they'd last that long.

Joshua eased the pain of those departing, took away their fears, and directed the souls to wait just outside the clinic where someone would escort them to heaven. He was drained of most of his energy by the time Julia collapsed.

Joshua caught her and held her until another nurse came along to help put her into a bed. He stayed by her side, his face a mixture of torment and love. He had no glow, no energy to help her hold on. He held her hand in one of his, the other he pressed to her cheek. When she exhaled her last breath, he staggered from the room to the stairwell and collapsed, sobbing.

Hers was the last soul he felt depart.

*****

Christian checked the clock. Still only 6:15 A.M. The only word from Ariel was a brief message saying the new planets were doing just lovely. Christian smiled at the words. He knew Ariel was glorified when allowed free rein over new ecosystems and would be a veritable bundle of energy the next time they met, vibrating with passion and an earthy scent he found oddly attractive. He never knew what to expect from Ariel's ever-changing form. Ariel was Ariel, whether light or dark, male or female. Ariel was his, and he was Ariel's. He smiled to himself. Love is love. Souls need no further definition.

Gabriel was busy keeping an ear open to the public outcry, news coverage, political maneuverings and rhetoric. Assisted by one hundred guardians, he worked tediously calming the panic and forestalling any outcries of one country against another. If he had his way, peace would finally smack all the politicians on the head. With an electrified flyswatter. Gabriel himself was an unmovable fixture in the UN headquarters in New York.

Chamuel materialized abruptly in the apartment.

"Cham! You didn't need to come down. I know you're helping Azrael –"

Chamuel waved him off. "There's something

wrong!"

"Well, the suicides have definitely stopped. Perhaps that's the imbalance you've felt shift," Christian suggested, and raised his eyebrows in question.

"No, it's something else. Where's Joshua and –" Chamuel stopped, looking away to the door to the apartment.

Michael materialized at that exact moment. "Joshua isn't answering my messages," he said. His manner brusque and irritated.

Christian pointed to the bedroom. He lifted his eyebrows and nodded his head. "Last night they..."

Michael and Chamuel looked in the direction of the bedroom and froze.

Chamuel was the first to recover. He strode quickly down the hall and threw the door to the bedroom open. "They're not here!" He raced back to the kitchen.

"Christian, check in with Uriel. See if Joshua is in his Office!" Michael was motioning his hands for him to hurry. He barely kept his impatience in check as Christian keyed in a query to Uriel.

[No, I haven't heard from him in some time.] Uriel followed that with a simple question mark. [?]

"The clinic?" Christian looked at Michael, starting to absorb his sense of panic.

Azrael arrived in the kitchen just as Michael and Christian were about to bolt out the door.

Christian stumbled and cried out, "Oh, no, oh,

please no." Christian collapsed to his knees.

Michael staggered and fell against the door, holding on to it in order to remain upright. "Oh, Josh, what have you done?"

Azrael fell into one of the kitchen chairs.

Chamuel stood rigid but swayed as if struck by powerful invisible waves buffeting him from all directions.

"Azrael, the clinic. Find him. Holy hell, this can't be happening." Christian turned shattered eyes to Michael. "I am not ready."

Azrael vanished and rematerialized at the clinic. Guardians were collecting souls. There were too many for Azrael to... he shook his head at himself. Focus, Az, you've got to find Joshua. He allowed himself to be noticed by only one nurse. Azrael touched her briefly. "Where is Julia Altieri?" He hoped Joshua wouldn't leave her. No, he will be wherever she is, I know it.

"She took ill. She's down –" The nurse blinked as Azrael took firmer control over her. "Follow me." She led him down one floor, through several hallways.

"Please, hurry, miss. It's very important I find her," Azrael fought the urge to pick her up and run with her football style.

They entered a room filled with partitioned-off beds. "Thank you," he said when he saw the bed where Julia lay. He already knew he was too late, her soul hovered above the bed. He looked frantically turned to his desk and began entering the program which would protect them on Earth and altered the New Program accordingly.

His role had just begun.

***

They chose a small section of land in the Bitterroot Mountains of Montana. Just west of Rivulet, off a small dirt road, a winding narrow driveway led back into a valley. There they placed a tidy cabin, complete with stone hearth and a wide porch, just the way Julia imagined. There was plenty of room to expand the cabin, and Christian was sure Joshua would have plenty of ideas for additions. It had been a while since he had tried his hand at carpentry, but his mind would retrain his body to do what had once been his first occupation. Learned at the side of his first earthly father.

Joshua watched with pleasure as Julia's eyes took in the scene. She's happy, he thought. Truly happy. He brought their entwined fingers to his lips, and he smiled at the sparkle in her eyes. "I take it you like it?" he asked, his voice teasing.

"Of course, I do. I love it!" She leaned in and tucked her head against his shoulder and sighed. After a minute, she let go of him and approached Christian. She drew him to her, held him fiercely. No words were needed between mother and son. She knew his plan and approved. She drew his head down and placed a kiss on his forehead. "My boy." It was enough to bring tears to both their eyes. Tears of good-bye. For now. With a nod she stepped away to allow Joshua to also say his goodbyes.

"Christian, please, do not be sad. Be happy for us," he said, holding Christian tight one last time. Joshua tried to remain in control of his own emotions. "I love you, son. And you are ready for this. I should know, I trained you. Be strong. Try not to drive Michael too crazy. Shake him up once in a while for me, though."

Christian nodded and smiled through tears.

"We will all be together again, son."

Joshua turned from him and embraced Michael. "Look after him. Like you did me."

Michael nodded. "You know I will. Take care of yourself." He looked at Julia, and said, "You think you could finally teach him to swim?" He smiled at both of them, unable to speak further.

Joshua stepped away and joined hands with Julia, and they turned to face their new home. At his nod, Azrael lay a hand on each, and altered their memories of the Program according to Christian's stipulations. He held them in stasis a moment longer, blinked back tears, and let them go.

Azrael, Michael and Christian watched as Joshua and Julia entered the cabin and closed the door.

"Merged souls should never be torn apart," Azrael said. "His father thought it would make him stronger. He couldn't have been more wrong." Azrael sighed, and looked at Christian and Michael. "Are you two going back up?"

"We'll join you shortly," Christian answered. He nodded to Azrael and waited until he dematerialized.

Michael was still contemplating the cabin. "I thought Joshua would make it through this. At least until the new Program was ready."

"It's my fault," Christian said. "I overestimated what he could endure."

"What if he doesn't want to stay here... to run the program?" Michael asked.

"It wasn't his soul I tied into Earth's new program."

Michael smiled and nodded his approval. "He'll stay."

"I doubt either will let the other out of their sight ever again," Christian said. "What about you, Michael? Have you decided?"

"I'll stay with them. You know what he's capable of on his own," he said. "Do you think she'll tell him?"

"That he didn't emerge the dominant soul? No, I don't think so." Christian said. "But I doubt he'd care."

"When do you want to launch the new code?" Michael asked.

Christian smiled. "Let's give Earth a few decades, first. See what its people come up with to explain the pandemic, see what changes they come up with. By then, I should have the kinks worked out of the Program. So far, Ariel's pleased with how it's working on Ravendune."

ABOUT THE AUTHOR

Jennifer A Dege

Jennifer has zigzagged all over the US... in a van... full of show dogs, collecting stories and scribbling poetry on the back on show entry envelopes. She has a teenage son, 2 dogs, and lives in rural Minnesota. The cats belong to the kid.

Thank you for reading Will You Know My Name? Please kindly consider leaving a brief review or rating on Amazon or Goodreads, as this allows other readers to find my books. Peace and love to you all...

Will You Know My Name? lays the foundations for the Souls Adrift series. Follow Christian, Michael, Joshua and others as they set up New Programs for New Planets and encounter other lost souls.

Novels COMING SOON:
Volume 2 - Reality Benders
Violume 3 - Soul Thieves

Made in the USA
Monee, IL
30 June 2020

33987446R00090